CW01501680

CHAPTER 1

My stomach growled loud enough to scare away the rabbit I'd been tracking for the past hour. Damn it.

"Come back here," I muttered, pushing myself up from my crouch and ignoring the way my joints cracked in protest. Six months in the wilderness hadn't made me a better hunter—just a more desperate one.

The rabbit darted between the snow-covered pines, its white coat blending perfectly with the terrain. I tracked its movement, forcing my weakened legs to move faster. One rabbit wouldn't sustain me for long, but it would quiet the gnawing emptiness that had become my constant companion since Callan had rejected me.

The memory of that day still burned like an open wound. His cold gray eyes as he'd looked me over, finding me wanting. *"You're too weak to be my mate,"* he'd declared, loud enough for every member of the Silverclaw Pack to hear. *"I need someone who will make me stronger, not drag me down."*

I'd felt our bond—the one that was supposed to be

MOUNTAIN MAN'S BABY

AN MPREG ROMANCE

IRONCLAW WOLVES
BOOK 1

ASHLYN DUPREE

CONTENTS

unbreakable—shatter like glass, each shard embedding itself into my heart. Physical pain had followed the emotional, rejection sickness settling into my bones like poison. My wolf had howled, broken and confused, as the mate chosen by fate himself denied what should have been.

My pack—former pack—had made their loyalties clear. When their rising alpha had publicly declared me unworthy, they'd watched in silence. No one had protested when I was driven beyond pack borders, left to survive a harsh mountain winter on my own.

Six months ago, I might have given up. Now? Spite was a surprisingly effective motivator.

I pushed wet auburn hair from my eyes, focusing on the rabbit's trail in the snow. My breath came in sharp pants, visible in the frigid air. I was close. So close—

A new scent cut through the crisp pine, and I froze.

Predator. Not wolf. Something worse.

I spun just as five hundred pounds of mountain lion launched from a nearby ledge, its massive body slamming into mine. I hit the ground hard, breath exploding from my lungs. Pain bloomed across my back as sharp claws tore through my threadbare shirt, catching on skin.

Perfect. If starvation didn't kill me, being mauled by an oversized cat would.

"Not today," I snarled, omega instincts screaming to submit, to go limp, but pride and stubbornness overruled them. I wasn't dying here, not after surviving alone for months. Not after everything I'd endured.

I twisted beneath the mountain lion, kicking upward into its belly. The cat yowled, momentarily startled by my resistance, and I used the brief reprieve to scramble backward, searching for anything I could use as a weapon.

My fingers closed around a hefty fallen branch. Not

much against several hundred pounds of predator, but better than bare hands.

The mountain lion recovered quickly, stalking toward me with deadly intent, pupils blown wide. I backed up until my spine pressed against a massive pine trunk. Nowhere left to run.

"Let's get this over with," I muttered, exhaustion making me reckless. I raised the branch, muscles aching with the effort. My body – once strong despite my omega status – had withered during these months alone. Rejection sickness had ravaged me from the inside out, making each day a battle just to keep breathing. The mountain lion's muscles bunched, preparing to pounce.

The attack I expected never came.

A blur of motion—impossibly fast—intercepted the mountain lion mid-leap. The two forms tumbled across the snow in a violent clash of fur and fury, spraying white powder in all directions. Blood spattered across the pristine snowbank—whose, I couldn't tell.

I blinked, trying to process what I was seeing. My rescuer wasn't fully shifted, caught somewhere between man and wolf. Massive shoulders. Dark hair. Savage grace in every movement.

Alpha. Undeniably, overwhelmingly alpha.

The scent hit me next – pine and smoke and something wild that made my wolf stir for the first time in months. Power radiated from him in waves, but not like Callan's showy dominance. This was deeper. More assured. The kind of strength that didn't need to prove itself.

The mountain lion swiped at the wolf-man's face, drawing crimson lines across his jaw. He didn't even flinch. Instead, he caught the cat's paw mid-strike and twisted. The sickening crack of breaking bone echoed through the trees, followed by the cat's pained shriek.

"Get out of here," the alpha growled, his voice deeper than the winter night and twice as cold, yet there was control in his rage – a precision to his violence that spoke of experience.

The mountain lion hesitated, weighing its odds, then apparently decided a half-starved omega wasn't worth the fight. It slunk away, favoring its injured leg, casting one last hateful glare at us before disappearing into the forest.

Only then did my rescuer turn toward me, and our eyes locked. Silver met gold.

The world seemed to tilt beneath my feet. Something electric passed between us, a recognition that went beyond conscious thought. My omega instincts, dulled by months of rejection sickness, suddenly flared to life, sending a jolt through my system that was almost painful in its intensity.

Mate.

The word whispered through me unbidden, and terror followed close behind. No. Not again. I wouldn't survive another fated mate bond, not after what Callan had done. The universe couldn't be cruel enough to tie me to another alpha who would inevitably find me wanting.

I gripped my pathetic branch tighter and lifted my chin. "Stay back."

The alpha approached anyway, but slowly, his hands slightly raised. Blood trickled down his jaw where the mountain lion had caught him. His silver eyes never left mine, and I could see the same shock in them – the recognition of what we were to each other.

"You're hurt," he said, his voice unexpectedly gentle for someone his size. "Let me help you."

"I've been managing on my own just fine," I replied, the

lie obvious to both of us. My side was on fire where the mountain lion's claws had raked me, and the familiar light-headedness of blood loss was setting in.

His gaze raked over my body, taking in my too-thin frame, the torn clothes, the exhaustion evident in every line of my posture. "Clearly," he said dryly.

I glared at him. "Thanks for the assist, but I'll be going now." I tried to push away from the tree, to demonstrate that I could stand perfectly well on my own, thank you very much—but my traitor legs buckled.

The alpha moved with startling speed, catching me before I hit the ground. The moment his skin touched mine, a current seemed to pass between us—warm, alive, undeniable. I gasped, unprepared for the intensity of it. The bond that had been severed with Callan seemed to reach hungrily toward this stranger, seeking to heal what had been broken.

"Let me go," I protested, pushing against his chest. Like trying to move a mountain. My wolf, meanwhile, wanted to burrow closer, to sink into the first real warmth we'd felt in months.

"I'm Kieran," he said, ignoring my struggle. "My cabin's not far."

"Didn't ask," I shot back, still pushing ineffectively against him. "And I don't need—"

"Help?" he finished for me. "The blood trail you're leaving suggests otherwise."

I glanced down. Sure enough, my side was bleeding freely where the mountain lion's claws had caught me. I hadn't even felt it in the rush of adrenaline.

"It's nothing," I insisted, though the edges of my vision were already growing fuzzy. The last thing I needed was to be in debt to an alpha – especially one whose very presence was stirring feelings I'd sworn never to feel again.

Kieran made a sound that might have been a laugh, though there was no humor in it. "Stubborn omega," he muttered, but there was something like respect in his tone.

Before I could muster an appropriately scathing response, he scooped me into his arms as if I weighed nothing. A protest died on my lips as my head spun, the blood loss and exhaustion finally catching up to me.

"Put me down," I said, but the words lacked conviction even to my own ears. The warmth of him was seeping into my perpetually cold body, and some traitorous part of me wanted to sink into it forever.

"When we reach the cabin," Kieran replied, already striding through the forest with unerring confidence. "What's your name?"

I hesitated. Names had power. But he'd already seen me at my weakest—what more damage could he do?

"Rowan," I conceded reluctantly.

Something flickered across his face—recognition? Satisfaction? Before I could decipher it, he nodded once. "Rowan," he repeated, as if testing how the name felt on his tongue.

My wolf stirred again, responding to the sound of my name on his lips. It had been so long since anyone had called me by name instead of "omega" or "weakling" or "reject." The last person to say it had been Callan, and he'd made it sound like a curse.

"How long have you been out here alone?" Kieran asked, his pace steady and sure as he navigated through the trees.

I didn't want to answer, didn't want to reveal just how pathetic my existence had become, but exhaustion loosened my tongue. "Six months," I admitted. "Since the rejection."

His arms tightened fractionally around me, a growl building in his chest. I stiffened, expecting anger directed at me, but instead he said, "Six months in these mountains, through autumn into winter, and you're still alive? That's not weakness, Rowan. That's strength."

I blinked in surprise. I'd survived because I'd had no choice, because giving up would have meant Callan was right about me. I'd never once thought of it as strength.

"I don't need saving," I mumbled against his chest, fighting to stay conscious. The steady rhythm of his heartbeat was strangely hypnotic, my body responding to his proximity in ways I couldn't control.

Kieran's arms tightened around me. "Everyone needs saving sometimes," he replied. "Even alphas."

The steady rhythm of his stride and the warmth of his body were pulling me toward unconsciousness. I fought it, wary of being completely vulnerable in an alpha's arms. My experiences had taught me that vulnerability was just another word for target.

"If you try anything," I warned, the threat comically ineffective given my current state.

"I don't take what isn't freely given," Kieran said, his voice hard with conviction. "I'm not that kind of alpha."

I'd heard similar promises before. Callan had once sworn to cherish me forever, to protect and treasure the mate fate had given him. Empty words, all of them.

"All alphas are the same," I murmured, darkness creeping in at the edges of my vision. My body was shutting down, the combination of starvation, cold, and fresh wounds too much to battle any longer.

Kieran slowed his stride just long enough to look down at me, his silver eyes intense. "I'm not him," he said quietly, and something in his tone made me believe he knew exactly who I was thinking about. "I'm not him, Rowan."

CHAPTER 2

I cradled the unconscious omega against my chest, trying to ignore the way my wolf howled within me, desperate to protect what was mine. His scent—pine needles and wild berries with an undercurrent of fear—filled my nostrils, triggering every protective instinct I possessed.

My cabin was less than a mile away, but the journey felt eternal with the wounded man in my arms. Every labored breath, every small whimper that escaped his cracked lips, drove daggers into my heart.

Mine. Protect. Mine.

My wolf wouldn't stop the primal chant, even as I tried to calm it. This omega—this stranger—needed help, not another alpha forcing claims upon him. The mountain lion's claws had left angry red streaks across his side, but what truly concerned me was how little he weighed in my arms. Beneath the torn clothes, his ribs were clearly visible, his cheekbones too sharp under pale, freckled skin.

"Just hold on," I murmured, quickening my pace as the

first snowflakes began to fall from the darkening sky. "We're almost there."

The omega stirred slightly, his wild auburn hair falling across his face as he mumbled something unintelligible. Then his golden eyes fluttered open for a brief moment, unfocused and glazed with fever.

"No... alpha," he whispered, his voice breaking. "Please... no more."

The raw fear in those words froze my blood. What had this omega endured to cause such terror? Who had hurt him so deeply that even unconscious, he fought against an alpha's touch?

"I won't hurt you," I promised, knowing he probably couldn't hear me. "You're safe now."

His eyes slipped closed again, his body going limp once more. I pushed myself faster, breaking into a jog despite the treacherous mountain path. Relief flooded through me when my cabin finally came into view—a solid timber structure nestled against the mountainside, smoke still curling from the chimney where I'd left my morning fire banked.

Inside, I gently laid the omega on my bed. Up close, in the warm light of the cabin, I could see the full extent of his condition. Beyond the mountain lion's attack, his body bore older marks—faded bruises and scars that spoke of a harsh life. But what struck me most was the emptiness I sensed—the hollow absence where a bond should have been.

This omega had been rejected. My alpha instincts roared in outrage. A rejection was the cruelest fate for an omega—a severing of a sacred bond that left permanent damage to body and soul.

"What kind of monster would do this to you?" I whispered, carefully cutting away the tattered remains of his shirt to assess his wounds.

The omega stirred again, this time more violently. "Weak," he mumbled, his face contorting with pain that seemed deeper than physical. "Too weak... not worthy..."

My hand stilled. Those weren't his words—they were echoes of what someone had said to him. The rejection hadn't just been physical; it had been deliberately cruel.

"You're not weak," I said firmly, though I knew he couldn't hear me. "You survived alone in these mountains. That takes more strength than most alphas possess."

Working methodically, I cleaned his wounds, applying the healing salve that Sawyer had given me before my retreat. The omega's skin burned with fever under my touch, and occasionally he would flinch or whimper, trapped in whatever nightmares haunted him.

"Callan... please," he begged in his delirium. "I can be... better. Stronger."

Callan. I committed the name to memory, a growl building in my throat. The name of my new enemy—who had taken this beautiful creature and broken him.

Once the wounds were bandaged, I turned my attention to the omega's other needs. I heated broth on the stove, knowing the starved man would need something gentle on his stomach. As I worked, I kept finding my gaze drawn back to the bed, to the pale figure who had somehow stumbled into my solitude and upended everything.

The fact that this was my fated mate wasn't lost on me. I'd felt it the moment our eyes met in the forest—that instant, undeniable pull that legends spoke of. But unlike the alpha who had rejected him, I would never force this bond nor would I ever reject it.

When the broth was ready, I returned to the bedside, gently lifting his head.

"You need to drink," I said softly, pressing the rim of the cup to his parched lips.

To my surprise, his eyes fluttered open—truly open this time, sharp with awareness despite the fever. Golden eyes, like sunlight through amber, stared up at me with a mixture of fear and defiance.

"Who—" His voice cracked, his throat too dry to form words.

"My name is Kieran," I said, keeping my voice low and soothing. "I found you being attacked by a mountain lion. You're in my cabin now. You're safe."

His eyes darted around the room, assessing escape routes. I recognized the look—it was the same wariness I'd seen in wolves who had been hunted too long.

"Drink," I said again, offering the broth. "Please. You need your strength."

After a moment's hesitation, he parted his lips, allowing me to tip a small amount of broth into his mouth. He swallowed with difficulty, but his eyes never left my face, watching for any sign of threat.

"Rowan," he whispered after a few sips. "My name."

Rowan. The name settled in my chest, feeling right in a way few things ever had.

"Rest, Rowan," I said. "Nothing will harm you here."

But his gaze hardened, a spark of that stubborn will that had kept him alive gleaming through the fever.

"Why are you... helping me?" he asked, each word clearly taking effort. "What do you... want?"

The suspicion in his voice cut deep, but I understood it. An omega alone in the wilderness, already betrayed by one alpha—trust would not come easily.

"I want nothing from you," I said honestly. "Except for you to heal."

Rowan's face twisted with disbelief. "Everyone wants... something."

I set the cup aside and moved back slightly, giving him space. "Not everyone is like the alpha who hurt you, Rowan."

The words struck like lightning. His eyes widened, then narrowed to slits, his scent spiking with panic.

"You don't know..." he began, trying to push himself up, only to fall back with a pained gasp as his wounds protested.

"I know enough," I said gently. "I can sense the rejection. But that's all I need to know for now. The rest is yours to share if you ever choose to."

He stared at me, confusion warring with the ingrained fear on his face. He was clearly unused to an alpha who didn't demand, who didn't take.

"Why?" he whispered again.

I considered my next words carefully. I could feel our bond humming between us, a silver thread connecting wolf to wolf, alpha to omega, but I wouldn't mention it. Not yet. Not when he was so wounded by the last bond that had been forced upon him.

"Because no one deserves to be thrown away," I said finally. "Because you're fighting so hard to survive. Rest now. We can talk more when your fever breaks."

His eyelids drooped, the brief surge of energy fading as exhaustion reclaimed him. Just before he drifted off, he murmured something that sounded like, "Don't... trust..."

"You don't have to trust me yet," I whispered, pulling the blanket up to his chin. "Just let me help you."

Throughout the night, I tended to him. His fever raged, bringing nightmares that had him thrashing against invisible demons. I changed his bandages when needed, coaxed broth and water between his lips whenever he was lucid enough to swallow, and kept the cabin warm against the growing storm outside.

All the while, I fought my own battle—against the alpha instincts that demanded I claim him, mark him, erase the scent of the alpha who had hurt him. My wolf paced restlessly inside me, furious that our mate bore another's rejection.

But I had seen the fear in Rowan's eyes. I had heard his broken pleas. This wasn't about what my wolf wanted; it was about what Rowan needed.

Dawn was breaking, pale light filtering through the cabin windows, when Rowan's fever finally broke. I was dozing in the chair beside the bed when a soft sound woke me. Opening my eyes, I found him watching me, his golden gaze clear for the first time since I'd found him.

"You're still here," he whispered, surprise evident in his voice.

"Of course I am," I replied, straightening. "How do you feel?"

"Like I was mauled by a mountain lion," he said, the ghost of wry humor in his voice.

I couldn't help the small smile that tugged at my lips. "Well, you're not wrong."

He tried to sit up, wincing as the movement pulled at his wounds. I moved to help him, but he flinched away from my outstretched hand. The small movement spoke volumes.

"Sorry," I said, pulling back immediately. "I should have asked first."

Confusion flickered across his face again. "You're... different."

"Different from what?"

"From other alphas," he said, his voice gaining strength but remaining guarded. "From him."

The way he said "him" told me everything I needed to know about who he meant. Callan. The alpha who had rejected him.

"I'm not him," I said simply. "I don't know what he did to you beyond the obvious, but I'm not him. I don't take what isn't mine."

His brow furrowed, disbelief plain on his face. "Then what do you want from me?"

I considered lying, telling him I wanted nothing at all. But something told me Rowan had been lied to enough.

"Right now? I want you to heal. To eat. To rest," I said. "And when you're stronger, I want you to decide what you want for yourself."

"And if I want to leave?" he challenged, chin lifting slightly.

"Then you can leave," I said, though the words physically hurt to say. My wolf howled in protest at the very idea. "But you need rest first. And the storm outside isn't making it any easier."

As if to punctuate my words, a gust of wind rattled the cabin windows, carrying the sound of heavy snowfall.

For a long moment, Rowan just stared at me, searching for the trap in my words. Then, very quietly, he said, "I don't understand you."

I smiled slightly. "You don't have to. Just know that while you're here, you're safe."

His eyes remained wary, but some of the tension eased from his shoulders. "I should thank you. For saving me."

"You fought well," I said honestly. "Most would have given up against a predator that size."

A bitter smile touched his lips. "I'm used to fighting losing battles."

The words struck a chord deep within me, stirring both

anger at what he had endured and admiration for his resilience.

"Get some more rest," I said, standing. "I'll make you something to eat."

I turned to go, but his voice stopped me.

"Kieran?"

I looked back, struck anew by how perfectly right his scent seemed in my home, how natural it felt to have him in my space.

"Yes?"

"I'm..." He paused, struggling with words that clearly didn't come easily. "I'm not good at being helped."

I'll never be like the alpha who hurt you. I'll show you that being wanted isn't the same as being owned. And if it takes forever, I'll wait. Because you're worth waiting for.

CHAPTER 3

I dreamt of Callan for the first time in months.

Not the Callan who had rejected me, his cold gray eyes dismissing me as worthless in front of our entire pack. No, I dreamt of the Callan I'd believed in—the one who'd smiled at me when our fated mate bond first sparked to life, the one who'd promised me the world.

"You were always meant to be mine," he whispered in the dream, reaching for me.

I backed away. "You threw me away."

His handsome face twisted with that familiar cruelty. "Because you were weak. Unworthy."

"No," I said, finding my voice stronger than it had ever been when facing him in reality. "You were wrong about me."

Dream-Callan lunged forward, hands reaching for my throat—

I jerked awake with a gasp, heart pounding. The cabin was dark except for the dim glow of banked coals in the fireplace. Rain, I realized. Not inside but outside, pattering against the roof where snow had fallen earlier. The storm was changing.

"Rowan?"

I nearly jumped out of my skin at the voice. Kieran materialized from the shadows, his silver eyes reflecting what little light remained like a wolf's.

"Sorry," he said, softer now. "I heard you. Nightmare?"

I nodded, not trusting my voice. The dream had felt so real—Callan's scent, his voice, the hatred in his eyes.

Kieran approached slowly, as if worried he might spook me. "Want to talk about it?"

"No," I said quickly. Then, because he'd been nothing but kind, I added, "Just... memories."

He nodded, accepting this without pressing. "The storm's shifting. Rain now. It'll clear by morning."

Morning. When I would leave. When I'd be alone again.

"Thank you," I said suddenly. "For helping me. You didn't have to."

Kieran's expression softened in the dim light. "Yes, I did," he replied simply.

Something in his tone made my chest tighten. "Why?"

He was silent for so long I thought he wouldn't answer. Finally, he said, "Because when I saw you fighting that mountain lion—half-starved, exhausted, alone—but still fighting..." He shook his head. "I've never seen such strength."

I scoffed. "I'm not strong. I'm just too stubborn to die."

"That is strength, Rowan."

The way he said my name sent a shiver down my spine that had nothing to do with cold.

"Get some more rest," he continued. "Tomorrow will be here soon enough."

As he turned to leave, I found myself saying, "Kieran?"

He paused, looking back over his shoulder.

"Why were you out there alone? Don't alphas usually have packs?"

A ghost of a smile touched his lips. "I have a pack. I just... needed space."

"From what?"

"Expectations," he replied cryptically. "Sleep well, Rowan."

MORNING BROUGHT NOT the clear sky Kieran had predicted, but a fresh onslaught of snow—thick, heavy flakes that fell in silent fury beyond the frost-rimmed windows.

I stood at the cabin's front window, the blanket Kieran had given me wrapped tightly around my shoulders, staring at the wall of white. My heart sank. I couldn't leave. Not in this.

"I've seen worse," I muttered to myself, trying to gather my resolve. Six months in the wilderness had hardened me. I'd survived rain, snow, wind—surely I could manage this.

But my body betrayed me at the thought, a violent shiver coursing through me. I was still weak, still recovering. The mountain lion's claws had left three parallel gashes down my side that burned when I moved too quickly. And though Kieran's food and shelter had begun to restore me, I knew the truth—I wasn't strong enough. Not yet.

Behind me, I heard Kieran moving in the kitchen area. The rhythmic sound of a knife hitting a cutting board. The soft sizzle of something in a cast-iron pan. Warm, mouthwatering scents filled the cabin—meat, herbs, the promise of another meal I hadn't had to hunt or scavenge for myself.

I hated how my stomach growled in response. How my

body seemed to know instinctively that this alpha would provide for me. That he would keep me safe.

No one keeps you safe but you, I reminded myself harshly. *Alphas don't protect; they own.*

But even as I thought it, my mind flashed to Kieran charging fearlessly at the mountain lion, placing himself between the predator and me without hesitation. How he'd tended my wounds with gentle hands that never lingered inappropriately. How he'd given me his bed and slept on a pallet by the fire.

"The storm's gotten worse," Kieran said, breaking the silence. His deep voice sent another involuntary shiver through me—one I desperately hoped he didn't notice. "You're welcome to stay until it passes."

I turned to face him, keeping the blanket clutched around me like armor. "How long?"

He glanced out the window, his expression thoughtful. "Hard to say. Three days, maybe more."

"More?" The word came out sharper than I intended. Panic fluttered in my chest. Three days trapped in this small cabin with an alpha—with my treacherous body already responding to his presence in ways I couldn't control.

Kieran's eyes locked with mine, and for a heartbeat, I could have sworn I saw the same panic reflected there. But then it was gone, replaced by that frustrating calm that seemed his natural state.

"I know it's not ideal," he said carefully. "But trying to leave in this would be suicide."

I knew he was right, but admitting it felt like surrender. "I can take care of myself."

"I'm sure you can." No condescension in his tone, just simple acknowledgment. "But there's no shame in waiting out a storm."

I turned back to the window, watching the snow pile higher against the glass. "I don't want to impose."

The floorboards creaked as he moved closer, stopping several feet away—always giving me space, never crowding. "You're not imposing, Rowan. I invited you."

"After saving me from a mountain lion," I muttered. "You didn't exactly have a choice."

"There's always a choice." Something in his voice made me look at him again. His silver eyes were steady, his face serious. "I could have left you in town with our pack healer. I could have taken you to the ranger station. I brought you here because I thought you'd be more comfortable somewhere quiet. Somewhere you could heal without..."

"Without a pack of wolves staring at the rejected omega?" I finished bitterly.

Kieran winced. "That's not what I was going to say."

"But it's true." I tightened the blanket around my shoulders. "I know what I am. What they'd think."

"My pack isn't like that," he said quietly.

I laughed, the sound harsh and hollow. "All packs are like that. Alphas rule, omegas serve. Or get discarded when they're not useful anymore."

Kieran was silent for a long moment. "Not all alphas," he finally said, so softly I barely heard him.

Something in his eyes made my chest tighten painfully. Before I could respond, he turned and walked back to the kitchen.

"Breakfast is almost ready," he called over his shoulder. "You should eat. Keep your strength up."

My first instinct was to refuse—to reject his care as stubbornly as I'd been rejected. But my stomach growled loudly, making the decision for me.

I approached the small wooden table cautiously. Kieran

set down two plates loaded with eggs, strips of venison, and what looked like pan-fried potatoes. The sight made my mouth water embarrassingly.

"Thank you," I said grudgingly, sitting down.

He nodded, taking the seat opposite me. "I'm not much of a cook, but it's edible."

I took a bite of the venison and had to stifle a moan. After months of barely surviving on whatever I could hunt or gather, this simple meal tasted like heaven. I devoured it quickly, my body desperate for nourishment.

When I looked up, I found Kieran watching me with a strange expression—somewhere between satisfaction and concern.

"What?" I asked defensively.

"Nothing," he said, looking away. "Just glad you're eating."

I pushed my empty plate away, suddenly self-conscious about how quickly I'd finished. "It was good. Thank you."

"There's more if you want it."

I hesitated, then shook my head. "I'm fine."

Kieran didn't push, just finished his own meal in comfortable silence. The snowstorm raged outside, but inside the cabin was warm, the fire crackling cheerfully in the hearth.

Against my will, I felt myself relaxing. The food, the warmth, the safety... it was dangerous how easily my body responded to these comforts. How much my omega instincts wanted to curl up by the fire and accept this alpha's protection.

He's not your alpha, I reminded myself harshly. *He's just being kind. Don't mistake kindness for something more.*

But even as I thought it, I caught him watching me again, his silver eyes reflecting the firelight. Something heated passed between us—something my body recognized even as my mind rejected it.

I stood abruptly, needing to put distance between us. "I should... I need some air."

Kieran raised an eyebrow. "In a blizzard?"

"Just on the porch," I clarified, already moving toward the door. "Just for a minute."

"Rowan—"

I didn't wait to hear his objection. I yanked open the door and stepped outside, the cold air hitting me like a physical blow. I gasped, the bitter wind stealing my breath as it whipped snow against my face. The blanket I'd brought provided almost no protection against the storm's fury.

But I didn't care. I needed to clear my head, to escape the confusing tangle of emotions this alpha stirred in me. The pull I felt toward him terrified me more than any mountain lion ever could.

I'd believed in the fated mate bond once before, and it had nearly destroyed me. I couldn't—wouldn't—make that mistake again.

I forced myself to take a step into the deeper snow of the yard, then another. My legs trembled beneath me, still weak from months of starvation and the recent attack. The wind howled around me, and the snow was already soaking through my borrowed clothes.

I can make it, I told myself desperately. *I survived worse than this. I can get away from here, away from him, before it's too late.*

But my traitor body had other ideas. My knees buckled, the world tilting sideways as exhaustion and cold overcame my determination. I was falling, the snow rising up to meet me—

Strong arms caught me before I hit the ground. Kieran's

scent enveloped me, pine and smoke and alpha, as he scooped me up against his chest.

"Let me go!" I struggled weakly, hating my body's betrayal, hating the way I instinctively turned into his warmth.

"So you can freeze to death?" he growled, his voice rumbling through his chest and into mine. "Not happening."

He carried me back inside, kicking the door shut behind us. The cabin's warmth hit me like a wave, making my frozen skin prickle painfully as sensation returned.

Kieran didn't set me down. Instead, he carried me straight to the hearth, grabbing more blankets with his free hand before lowering me gently onto the thick bearskin rug before the fire.

"What were you thinking?" he demanded, wrapping the blankets around me with efficient movements. His face was tight with anger, but his hands remained gentle. "You're still recovering. You could have died out there."

I looked away, unable to meet his eyes. "I would have been fine."

"No," he said firmly, "you wouldn't have. And I'm not going to watch you kill yourself because you're too stubborn to accept help."

"I didn't ask for your help!" I snapped, anger replacing embarrassment. "I didn't ask to be saved! I didn't ask to be trapped here with you!"

"You'd rather I had left you to the mountain lion?" he asked quietly.

The question deflated my anger instantly. "No," I admitted reluctantly. "But I can't stay here."

"Why not?" Kieran knelt before me, close enough that I could feel the heat radiating from his body but still maintaining that careful distance. "What are you so afraid of, Rowan?"

"I'm not afraid," I lied.

He didn't call me on it, just watched me with those intense silver eyes that seemed to see straight through my defenses.

"It's the storm," he said finally. "Not me. You're not trapped with me; you're sheltering from weather that would kill you. As soon as it's safe, you can go wherever you want."

I wanted to believe him. Wanted to believe there was an alpha who wouldn't try to control me, own me, break me. But experience had taught me otherwise.

"Why are you doing this?" I asked, my voice barely a whisper. "Why help me? What do you want?"

Something flashed in Kieran's eyes—hurt, maybe, or frustration. "Not everything comes with a price, Rowan."

"Everything comes with a price," I countered. "Especially when an alpha is involved."

He was silent for a long moment. Then, with a sigh that seemed to come from deep inside him, he said, "I'm going to chop more firewood. The storm's getting worse, and we'll need it. Stay by the fire. Please."

He stood, grabbing his coat from a hook by the door.

"You're going out in this?" I asked, surprised.

Kieran paused at the door. "The woodshed's just behind the cabin. I'll be fine." He glanced back at me, his expression unreadable. "I won't be gone long. And Rowan?"

"Yes?"

"You're not going to die because some bastard didn't see your worth." He said and closed the door softly.

I stared after him, his words echoing in my mind.

Alone by the fire, wrapped in blankets that smelled of

him, I felt the first treacherous cracks forming in the walls I'd built around my heart. This pull, this recognition, this impossible connection—I couldn't fight it forever.

CHAPTER 4

The snowstorm outside the cabin had intensified, howling through the trees like a pack of wolves on the hunt. The wind rattled the windows, and the fire in the hearth flickered as if trying to keep up with the storm's fury. I huddled under the blankets, my body shivering not just from the cold, but from something deeper, something more primal that I'd been dreading since the moment Kieran had brought me to his cabin.

My heat was coming.

I could feel it building beneath my skin—the first unmistakable signs of my cycle. It was a sensation I had grown to dread, a reminder of my omega nature that had once been a source of pride but now felt like a curse. My skin felt too tight, my senses heightened to an almost painful degree. Every nerve ending tingled with awareness, and the wool blanket Kieran had wrapped around me now felt like sandpaper against my oversensitive skin.

I tried to hide it, burying my face in the pillow and willing the sensations away. The last thing I wanted was for

Kieran to notice. I couldn't bear the thought of him seeing me like this, vulnerable and needy. My ex-mate, Callan, had made it crystal clear that my omega nature was a weakness, something to be ashamed of.

"Disgusting," he'd called it once, when my heat had come early and interrupted an important pack gathering. "Control yourself. You're embarrassing me."

I clenched my eyes shut at the memory, trying to ignore the burning that had started deep in my core. It was impossible to hide though—my body was betraying me, responding to the primal call of nature. I could feel sweat beginning to bead on my forehead despite the chill in the air, and my breaths were coming faster, shallower. The heat was building rapidly, far quicker than I'd anticipated, my body's response to being in such close proximity to a compatible alpha after months of isolation.

The worst part was that my body instinctively wanted Kieran. Even now, my senses were attuned to his movements in the kitchen, the scent of cooking food mingling with his natural musk. Every sound he made—the clatter of pots, the soft hum under his breath—sent jolts of longing through me. I bit down hard on my lip to suppress the whimper that threatened to escape.

I heard Kieran pause in his movements, and even from across the cabin, I could sense the moment he caught my scent. My heat pheromones had to be filling the space by now, unmistakable to any alpha. I tensed, waiting for his reaction—waiting for the disgust, the mockery, or worse, the predatory interest I'd seen in other alphas' eyes before.

The sound of his footsteps approached my small corner of the cabin. Each step seemed to echo through my heightened senses. My heart raced so fast I thought it might burst from my chest. I kept my eyes tightly shut, not wanting to see whatever expression crossed his face.

"Rowan." His voice was tight, controlled. I couldn't read the emotion behind it.

I reluctantly opened my eyes to find him standing several feet away, his posture rigid. His silver eyes had darkened, his pupils dilated, but he was keeping his distance. His hands were clenched into fists at his sides, but he wasn't moving towards me.

"I'll get you water," he said, his voice rough. "And food. You'll need your strength."

I stared at him, confusion cutting through the fog of heat that was threatening to overtake my mind. "You're not—" I couldn't finish the thought.

Understanding flashed across his face. "No," he said firmly. "I will never hurt you."

He returned with a pitcher of water and a plate of food. He set them down beside me but maintained his distance. The effort it took him was visible—a slight tremor in his hands, the tightness around his eyes, the carefully controlled breathing.

"I need to leave," he said, voice strained. "Give you your privacy."

"You're leaving?" The words burst from me before I could stop them, edged with a panic that surprised even me. The thought of being alone, of facing the unbearable heat without anyone nearby, was suddenly terrifying.

Kieran misread my reaction. "I won't go far," he promised. "Just... outside. I'll sleep in the shed tonight." His eyes met mine, and I was shocked by the gentleness there. "You're safe here, Rowan. I don't take what isn't freely given."

With that, he grabbed his coat and headed for the door.

The blast of cold air as he opened it was a momentary relief against my feverish skin, but then he was gone, and I was alone with the roaring fire and the howling storm.

I lay there in shock, trying to process what had just happened. An alpha—a powerful, unmated alpha—had just walked away from an omega in heat. It defied everything I thought I knew about alphas. About what I deserved.

But as the minutes passed and my heat intensified, a new kind of agony took hold. My body, primed for mating, rebelled against the absence of an alpha. Cramps seized my abdomen, and I curled into myself, gasping at the intensity. Slick dampened my thighs, and the emptiness inside me became a physical ache so profound that tears sprang to my eyes.

Memories of Callan flooded back, vivid and cruel.

"Your heat is inconvenient," he'd said during our last cycle together, barely looking at me as he'd fulfilled his duty with clinical detachment. "Try to be quieter next time. Your neediness is pathetic."

I'd believed him. I'd believed myself weak, disgusting, unworthy of tenderness.

A particularly violent cramp tore through me, and I couldn't hold back a cry of pain. I pressed my face into the pillow, shame washing over me. This was what I was—what I'd always be. An omega slave to biology, to need, to weakness.

And yet... Kieran had walked away. Not because he didn't want me—his body's response had been clear enough—but because he respected me. Because he wouldn't take advantage of me.

Hours passed in a fever dream of need and pain. Night fell, and the storm showed no signs of abating. By midnight, I was delirious, my skin on fire, my clothes soaked with sweat. I'd thrown off the blankets, but nothing helped. The emptiness inside me had become a torment beyond endurance.

Each wave of need was stronger than the last. My body ached for relief, for completion—for him. I fought it, refusing to call out, to show that weakness. But my resistance was crumbling with each passing minute.

"Kieran..." His name escaped my lips like a prayer, a desperate plea that I couldn't contain anymore. "Please..."

I didn't expect him to hear me. I didn't expect him to come back through that door, facing the storm he'd fled to escape the torment of my scent. But as another wave of need crashed over me, so intense I couldn't stifle my cry, I heard the cabin door open.

Snow swirled in, carried by the howling wind. And there stood Kieran, silhouetted against the night, his silver eyes gleaming like a predator's in the dim light. His chest heaved with each breath, as if he'd been running. Or fighting some internal battle.

I should have been afraid. I should have retreated, protected myself from whatever was about to happen. But all I felt was relief. Pure, overwhelming relief.

"Kieran," I gasped, my voice breaking. "It hurts. Make it stop. Please..."

His eyes locked with mine, and in them I saw a mirror of my own desperation—desire barely leashed, need barely contained. He took one step forward, then another, his movements careful as if approaching a wounded animal.

"Are you sure, Rowan?" he asked, his voice a low growl that sent shivers down my spine. "I need to hear you say it."

In that moment, with the fire of need consuming me from within, there was only one possible answer.

"Yes," I whispered, reaching for him. "Yes, I'm sure. I need you. Please..."

Kieran crossed the room in three powerful strides, and as his scent enveloped me—pine and snow and pure alpha—I knew there was no turning back.

CHAPTER 5

I stood on the porch, the freezing wind whipping around me, but it was nothing compared to the heat coursing through my veins. Rowan's scent, rich with the intoxicating aroma of his heat, filled the air, driving my alpha instincts into overdrive. I gripped the railing until my knuckles turned white, my claws extending involuntarily as I fought to maintain control.

I could hear him inside, his soft moans and desperate whimpers echoing through the cabin walls. Each sound was a knife twisting in my gut, a primal call that beckoned me to go to him, to claim what every fiber of my being knew was mine. But I had promised him space, promised him that I wouldn't take what wasn't freely given. I wouldn't be like Callan.

I closed my eyes, trying to focus on the cold, the bite of the wind, anything to distract me from the overwhelming need to be with Rowan. But it was no use. His scent was everywhere, sweet, intoxicating, and laced with pain. The pain was what kept me rooted in place.

"Control yourself," I growled, my voice rough and unfamiliar even to my own ears. My wolf was too close to the surface, pushing against my skin, demanding to be released. Demanding to claim our mate.

Rowan's moans grew louder, more desperate. He was fighting it, fighting the urge to call out for me, but his body was betraying him. His omega instincts were too strong, too primal to be denied.

A particularly violent gust of wind drove snow into my face, the icy particles sticking to my eyelashes. I welcomed the cold, hoping it would clear my head, dull my senses. It didn't. If anything, the contrast between the frigid air and the heat within me only made me more aware of my body's demands.

Suddenly, Rowan's cries turned into sobs, raw and broken. The sound tore at my heart, shredding my resolve. I stepped towards the door, my hand shaking as I reached for the handle. I didn't turn it.

I leaned my forehead against the door, breathing heavily, fighting the urge to break it down. "Please, Rowan," I whispered, knowing he couldn't hear me. "Let me help you."

And then, through the storm and the wind, I heard it. His voice, barely above a whisper, but filled with desperation. "Kieran... please."

It was all I needed. I pushed the door open and stepped inside, my heart pounding in my chest. The cabin air was thick with his scent, so powerful it made my head spin. Rowan lay on the bed, his body trembling, his skin flushed and glistening with sweat. The thin sheet he'd wrapped around himself was damp and twisted, barely covering him. His golden eyes, bright with fever, locked onto mine, filled with a mix of fear and desperate need.

"Kieran," he gasped, his voice breaking. "Make it stop. Please."

I crossed the room in three strides, my heart aching for him. I knelt beside the bed, my hands reaching out to gently cup his face. He flinched at my touch, but I held him steady, my eyes locked onto his.

"Rowan," I said softly, fighting to keep my voice calm when everything in me wanted to growl with possession. "Are you sure? I need to hear you say it."

He hesitated for a moment, conflict clear in his eyes. The fear of another rejection battling with his body's desperate need. Then he nodded, his voice a broken whisper. "Please... I can't... I need you. It hurts too much."

I brushed a strand of sweat-soaked auburn hair from his forehead. "I'm here," I whispered, my thumb brushing away a tear from his cheek. "I won't hurt you. I promise." I meant it with every part of my being, even as my body shook with the effort to stay gentle, to not simply take him the way my instincts demanded.

He nodded, his breath hitching in his chest. I leaned in, my lips brushing softly against his. He tensed for a moment, then melted into the kiss, his body responding to mine. I deepened the kiss, my hands sliding down to his shoulders, then to his chest, feeling the rapid beat of his heart beneath my palm.

Rowan gasped as my hand moved lower, his body arching into my touch. "Alpha," he whispered, the word slipping out unbidden. I felt him freeze, panic flashing across his face at the admission.

"It's okay," I murmured against his lips. "You're safe with me." I kissed him again, deeper this time, pouring all my reassurance into it. His hands came up to grip my shoulders, his nails digging into my skin as if he was afraid I'd disappear.

I took my time, exploring his body with gentle touches

and soft kisses. I wanted him to feel cherished, to know that he was safe with me. His body responded to my touch, his breaths coming faster, his moans growing louder. The sweet scent of his arousal mixed with his heat pheromones, creating an intoxicating blend that made my head swim.

I slowly undressed him, my hands shaking slightly as I revealed his pale skin, marred by old scars and new bruises. I kissed each one, my heart aching for what he had endured. I wanted to erase every memory of hurt, to replace it with love and care.

"Kieran," he whimpered, his hips bucking upward involuntarily. "Please, I need—"

"Shh," I soothed, trailing kisses down his stomach. "I know what you need. Let me take care of you."

His body arched against mine, his need growing more urgent. I could feel his heat, his desire, like a living thing between us. I slid my hand down, my fingers finding his entrance, already slick and ready. He gasped as I gently pressed against him, his body opening for me without resistance, my fingers slipping inside.

He moaned, his body tightening around my fingers. I took my time, preparing him, making sure he was ready. His body was on fire, his need consuming him, but I wanted this to be perfect. I wanted him to know that he was loved, that he was wanted.

"Alpha," he cried out, his head thrashing on the pillow. "Please, I can't—I need you inside me."

I removed my own clothes, my movements urgent now. His scent was driving me wild, my wolf howling for release. But still, I held back, hovering over him, my eyes locked onto his. I saw the fear in his eyes, the uncertainty, but also the need, the desire. I leaned in, my lips brushing against his ear.

"You're mine," I whispered, my voice filled with promise. "And I will never hurt you. Do you understand?"

He nodded, his breath hitching in his chest. "Yours," he whispered back, the word seeming to surprise him as much as it did me.

I positioned myself at his entrance, the head of my cock pressing against him. I could feel how ready he was, how much he needed this, but still I hesitated, searching his face for any sign of doubt.

"Please," he begged, his hands sliding down to grip my hips, pulling me closer. "Kieran, I need you."

I slid into him slowly, carefully, feeling his body stretch to accommodate me. He gasped, his fingers digging into my shoulders, his body trembling beneath me. The tight heat of him was almost unbearable, and I had to grit my teeth to keep from thrusting wildly.

"Okay?" I managed to ask, my voice strained.

He nodded, his eyes squeezed shut, his bottom lip caught between his teeth. "More," he whispered.

I moved slowly at first, my body in tune with his, every thrust measured and controlled. His moans grew louder, his body responding to mine, his heat consuming us both. I could feel the bond between us, the connection that tied us together, growing stronger with every touch, every kiss.

"Kieran," he cried out, his nails raking down my back, leaving trails of fire in their wake. "More, please, harder."

I obeyed, my control slipping as my thrusts became deeper, more urgent. The bed creaked beneath us, the headboard slamming against the wall with each powerful drive of my hips. Rowan's legs wrapped around my waist, pulling me deeper, his body demanding everything I had to give.

"Mine," I growled, the word escaping without conscious thought. "My omega. My mate."

"Yours," he echoed, his voice breaking on a sob. "Alpha, please—I'm so close."

I could feel it too, the pressure building at the base of my cock. The knot beginning to form, the primal bond that would tie us together forever. I looked into his eyes, seeing the fear and the love, the need and the desire. And I knew, in that moment, that he was mine, and I was his.

"I'm going to knot you," I warned, my voice rough with desire. "Are you ready?"

His eyes widened, a flash of panic crossing his face. But then he nodded, his body arching into mine. "Yes," he gasped. "Make me yours, Alpha."

With one final thrust, I buried myself inside him, the knot swelling, locking us together. Rowan cried out, his body convulsing around mine, his release hitting him with the force of a tidal wave. I followed immediately, my orgasm ripping through me with an intensity I'd never experienced before. The mating bond between us flared to life, a tangible connection that bound our souls together as surely as our bodies.

The knot pulsed, wave after wave of pleasure washing over us both. I carefully maneuvered us onto our sides, still joined, his back against my chest. I held him close, my arms wrapped around him, my face buried in his neck, breathing in his scent—now marked with my own.

In the aftermath, we lay together, our bodies entwined, our breaths mingling. I held him close, my heart still racing, my body still trembling with the intensity of our connection. But as the minutes passed, I felt him grow tense, his body stiffening against mine.

"Rowan?" I whispered, my lips brushing against his shoulder. "What is it?"

He didn't answer immediately, but I could smell the

change in his scent—the sharp tang of fear and regret cutting through the lingering sweetness of pleasure. Finally, he turned his head, his eyes meeting mine, filled with tears.

"You took advantage of me," he whispered, his voice shaking. "You knew I couldn't resist."

His words cut through me like a knife, and I felt a surge of pain and anger. But I held it back, my voice steady as I looked into his eyes. "Rowan," I said softly, "I would never force you to do something you didn't want. You asked for me, remember?"

He shook his head, the movement dislodging a tear that tracked down his cheek. "I didn't want this," he said, his voice filled with regret. "I didn't want to be claimed again. My body betrayed me, that's all."

I wanted to argue, to point out how he'd responded to me, how he'd begged for more. But I knew that would only make things worse. Instead, I held him tighter, my heart aching for him.

"I'm not Callan," I whispered, my voice filled with promise. "I will never hurt you, Rowan. You have to believe that."

But as he looked at me, his eyes filled with fear and regret, I knew that it would take more than words to convince him. It would take time, patience, and love. And I was willing to give him all that and more. Because he was mine, and I was his. And nothing would ever change that.

"The heat made me weak," he said, his voice small and wounded. "It made me forget what happens when you give yourself to an alpha. They take, and take, until there's nothing left of you."

My heart shattered at his words, at the pain behind them. "Rowan," I said gently, cupping his face in my hands. "Look at me."

He did, reluctantly, his golden eyes swimming with tears.

I brushed them away with my thumbs, my touch as gentle as I could make it.

"I don't want to take from you," I told him, pouring every ounce of sincerity I possessed into my words. "I want to give. Protection. Safety. A home where you belong. A family who will never cast you out."

Doubt flickered across his face, but he didn't pull away. Progress, however small. "You say that now," he murmured, "but when the heat is gone and you see me for what I really am—"

"I already see you," I interrupted, pressing my forehead against his. "A survivor. Strong enough to endure what would have killed most wolves. Brave enough to fight a mountain lion when you barely had the strength to stand. That's who you are, Rowan. And that's who I want."

He closed his eyes, a fresh tear escaping. "You don't understand," he whispered. "Callan said the same things. Until he didn't."

The knot had gone down enough that I could separate us. I did so gently, then pulled him into my arms, his head resting on my chest. He was stiff at first, resistant, but gradually relaxed as I stroked his hair.

"Then I'll just have to prove it to you," I said quietly. "Day by day. For as long as it takes."

He didn't answer, but he didn't pull away either. And for now, that was enough. The bond between us was new, fragile as spun glass. But it was there. And I would protect it, nurture it, until he could trust in it as much as I did.

Because he was mine. My mate. My omega.

And I would never let him forget it again.

CHAPTER 6

I woke with a jolt, my body aching in places I'd forgotten could feel. For one blissful moment, I floated in the hazy space between dreams and reality —warm, safe, my body humming with a strange new contentment.

Then it all came rushing back.

The heat. The desperation. The begging.

Oh gods, the begging.

My face burned hot with shame—my hands clawing at Kieran's chest, my voice breaking as I pleaded for him to take me. I remembered the feral look in his silver eyes when he finally gave in, the way his sweaty body had covered mine, the searing pain and overwhelming pleasure of his knot locking us together.

My fingers trembled as they flew to my neck, finding the tender spot where his teeth had broken skin. The bond mark. The physical manifestation of what I'd allowed to happen.

What had I done?

Panic clawed up my throat, my chest tightening until

each breath became a struggle. I threw back the blankets, wincing at the soreness that radiated through my lower body.

I grabbed for my clothes, scattered across the floor in our desperation the night before. My hands shook so badly I could barely pull on my pants.

"Calm down," I whispered to myself, pressing my palms against my eyelids. "Think, Rowan. Think."

But thinking was impossible with Kieran's scent everywhere—in the sheets, on my skin, inside me. The bond mark pulsed with a strange warmth that made my stomach twist with confused longing. Part of me—the omega part I'd been fighting for so long—wanted to curl back into those blankets and wait for him to return. To surrender completely.

That was the part of me that had believed Callan, too.

The memory of my former love was like a bucket of ice water. Six months hadn't dulled the humiliation of standing before my entire pack as Callan spat at my feet and declared me unworthy. "You're too weak to be my mate," he'd said, his voice carrying for all to hear. "I need someone who will make me stronger, not drag me down."

My packmates' faces had blurred through my tears as they turned away one by one, following their alpha's lead. No one spoke for me. No one helped when I collapsed, the severing of our partial bond leaving me gasping on the ground like a fish thrown to shore.

I'd crawled away that night, dragging myself into the wilderness rather than face another day of their contempt. Better to die with dignity in the forest than live as the rejected omega, forever marked by failure.

And now I'd done it again. Given myself to an alpha who might just as easily decide I wasn't enough.

The sound of movement from the other room froze me in place. Kieran was awake. My heart hammered wildly as footsteps approached, each one making me flinch. Would he be different now that he'd gotten what he wanted? Now that the hunt was over and the prize claimed?

The bedroom door swung open, and Kieran filled the frame, massive and imposing. His dark hair was mussed from sleep, his jaw shadowed with stubble. The sight of him sent an involuntary shiver through me—part fear, part something else I refused to name.

His silver eyes locked onto mine, widening slightly at finding me half-dressed and clearly panicking.

"Rowan." My name on his lips was soft, careful. "Are you alright?"

I backed up instinctively until my shoulders hit the wall. "Stay back."

He didn't move, just tilted his head slightly. "You're afraid."

"I'm not afraid," I lied, my voice cracking. "I just... I need space."

"Alright." He raised his hands, palms out. "I'll keep my distance."

The easy surrender threw me. Callan would have snarled at such disrespect, would have used his alpha voice to force submission. Kieran just stood there, making himself smaller somehow despite his massive frame.

"I made breakfast," he said after a moment. "And there's coffee. You should eat something. The heat took a lot out of you."

My face flushed hot again at the mention of my heat. "Is that all you have to say? After what happened?"

A crease formed between his brows. "What would you like me to say?"

"I don't know!" I pushed away from the wall, agitation making it impossible to stand still. "Something! Anything! You claimed me. We're—" I couldn't say the word 'mated.' It stuck in my throat like a bone.

"Bonded," he finished quietly. "Yes."

"And you have nothing to say about it?" My voice rose, hysteria edging in. "Aren't you going to tell me what happens now? What you expect? What the rules are?"

Understanding dawned in his eyes. "Rowan, there are no rules. No expectations beyond what you're willing to give."

I laughed bitterly. "Right. Sure. All alphas say that, until they don't get what they want."

"I'm not all alphas." His voice remained infuriatingly calm. "And I'm certainly not him."

The mention of Callan, however indirect, made me flinch. "You don't know anything about that."

"I know enough." Kieran's eyes softened. "I know someone hurt you. Betrayed you. Made you believe you weren't worth fighting for."

My throat tightened painfully. "Maybe I wasn't."

"That's bullshit." For the first time, heat entered his voice, a low growl underlying the words. "You were always meant to be wanted, Rowan. Always."

Tears stung my eyes, and I blinked furiously to hold them back. "You can't know that."

"I do know it." He took a step forward, then stopped when I tensed. "I've known it since I first caught your scent on the wind. Since I saw you fighting that mountain lion with nothing but a stick and sheer stubbornness."

A flash of memory hit me—our eyes meeting in the forest, silver to gold, the world tilting beneath my feet. That electric current that had passed between us, recognition so deep it transcended conscious thought. My body had known him even as my mind rejected the possibility.

"My wolf recognized you immediately as our mate," Kieran continued, his voice dropping to a rumble that seemed to vibrate through my very bones.

"Then why did Callan reject me?" The question burst out before I could stop it, raw and bleeding. "If I was 'meant to be wanted,' why did my fated mate throw me away like garbage?"

Kieran's jaw tightened. "Because he was a fool who didn't deserve you."

"Or because he saw the truth," I whispered. "That I'm weak. Worthless."

"Stop." Kieran closed the distance between us in two long strides, his hands gripping my upper arms. "You survived six months alone in these mountains after enduring a severed bond that kills most omegas. You fought off predators. You hunted. You endured winter storms with nothing but your wits. There is nothing—nothing—weak about you."

I wanted to pull away, but my body betrayed me, leaning into his warmth. The bond mark on my neck pulsed, sending waves of warmth through my body. My wolf whined, recognizing its mate, wanting to submit, to be claimed again, to be safe.

"What if—" my voice broke. "What if you change your mind too?"

His hands gentled, sliding up to cup my face. "Rowan, look at me."

I did, reluctantly meeting those silver eyes that seemed to see straight into my soul.

"I would have waited forever if that's what you needed," he said, each word deliberate and weighted with sincerity. "I never intended to claim you during your heat. I fought against every instinct to give you time. But now that it's happened, now that you're mine—" His thumb brushed across my cheekbone. "I will never regret it. Not for a single moment."

I stared at him, searching for any hint of deception, any flicker of the cruelty I'd come to expect. There was none. Just that steady, unwavering gaze that promised things I was afraid to believe in.

"I can't," I whispered, pulling back from his touch. "I can't trust this. I can't trust you."

Something like pain flashed across his features, but he let his hands fall away. "I understand."

"No, you don't!" Frustration made my voice sharp. "You can stand there making promises because you have all the power! You're the alpha. You get to decide if I'm worth keeping or not."

"That's not how this works, Rowan. Not with me."

"Then how does it work?" I demanded, wrapping my arms around myself. "Because every instinct I have is screaming that this is too good to be true. That you'll turn on me the moment I believe you."

Kieran stepped back, something resolute settling in his expression. "You want to know how much power you have?" He strode to the door, yanking it open. The morning light spilled in, along with the crisp mountain air. "There it is. Your freedom. If you want to leave, you can walk through it right now, and I won't stop you."

I stared at him, then at the open door, my heartbeat thundering in my ears. "Just like that?"

"Just like that." His voice was steady, but I could see the effort it took in the rigid set of his shoulders, the slight tremor in his hands. The scent of distress rolled off him in waves, contradicting his calm facade. "I meant what I said. I would have waited forever. I still will, if that's what you need."

The bond mark on my neck pulsed painfully at the thought of walking away from him. We both knew what happened to mated pairs who separated—the physical agony, the hollow emptiness that would haunt us both. Yet he was offering me the choice anyway.

I moved slowly toward the door, watching his expression crumble slightly with each step. But I needed to know—needed to be sure this wasn't another trap.

As I neared the threshold, my body rebelled. The bond between us pulled taut, a physical sensation like a hook behind my navel. My wolf howled in protest at the mere thought of leaving our mate. Even my skin seemed to burn at the proximity to the doorway, as if warning me against crossing it.

"Why?" I whispered, one hand on the doorframe. "Why would you let me go when you could force me to stay?"

"Because a cage is still a cage, even if it's made of gold." His eyes held mine, fierce with conviction. "I don't want an omega who stays out of fear or obligation. I want a mate who chooses me, every day, because he wants to be here."

I felt the dam inside of me give way, a crack in the wall I'd built around my heart. My gaze drifted past him into the cabin—the cabin he'd been slowly adapting for me without my even noticing. A lower shelf in the kitchen I could reach without stretching. Extra blankets piled near the fire, knowing I was always cold. Books on the bedside table—books I'd mentioned once in passing that I'd enjoyed as a child.

This wasn't just Kieran's space anymore. It had been becoming mine too, in a hundred small ways I hadn't allowed myself to see.

"I don't understand you," I said, my hand falling from the doorframe.

A faint smile touched his lips. "You will. In time."

I looked at the open door one last time, at the freedom he was offering me. Then back at him. Slowly, deliberately, I pushed the door closed. "I'm not staying forever," I said, needing him to understand. "Just... for now. Until I figure things out."

He nodded, accepting my terms without argument. "For as long as you want."

"And I'm not promising anything," I added. "Just because we're bonded doesn't mean—"

"I know." His voice was gentle. "One day at a time, Rowan. That's all I'm asking for."

One day at a time. I could do that. Could give myself that much, at least.

"I made pancakes," he said after a moment, changing the subject with surprising grace. "They're probably cold now, but I can reheat them."

The normality of the offer—so domestic, so ordinary— struck me as absurd after the intensity of our conversation. "Pancakes? Really?"

He shrugged, a smile tugging at his lips. "I'm told my pancakes are worth staying for, at least for breakfast."

It wasn't a declaration of undying love. It wasn't even a promise that things would work out between us. But as I followed him to the kitchen, the bond mark a warm, steady pulse against my skin, I allowed myself to consider the possibility that maybe—just maybe—Kieran was right.

Maybe it was the mate bond pulling at my insides, the one I'd been fighting since the moment our eyes met in the forest, wasn't a trap but a compass pointing me home.

Maybe I was always meant to be wanted, after all.

CHAPTER 7

Something inside of me had changed. I couldn't identify what it was, but I knew I was different. I touched my stomach, fingers trembling against my skin. The sensation had been growing stronger each morning—a warm pulse that seemed to radiate outward from my center, like a tiny star taking root.

For days, I'd ignored the signs. The sudden aversion to the coffee Kieran brewed each morning. The dizziness when I stood too quickly. The way certain scents—pine, smoke, earth—had intensified until they almost overwhelmed me. The way other scents—the salted venison Kieran had prepared two nights ago—had sent me fleeing outside to gulp fresh air.

My body knew before my mind would accept it.

I swung my legs over the side of the bed, fighting back a wave of dizziness. The cabin was quiet; Kieran had gone out to check his snares. I was grateful for the moment alone as I padded to the bathroom, my bare feet cold against the wooden floor.

The face that stared back at me from the mirror was

barely recognizable. My cheeks had filled out in the weeks I'd been here. The hollowness beneath my eyes had faded, and my skin had lost the sickly pallor of starvation. My auburn hair had regained some of its luster, and my eyes—they seemed to glow now, the gold flecks more vibrant than I'd ever seen them.

I looked... alive. Healthy.

And somehow different.

I stripped off my borrowed sleep shirt—one of Kieran's, hanging loosely on my smaller frame but comforting in its lingering scent. With trembling fingers, I examined my body. My skin seemed to glow from within, taking on a warmth I'd never had before. My chest felt tender. And my stomach, while still flat, had a firmness to it that hadn't been there before.

I gripped the edge of the sink, a memory washing over me like ice water.

Callan's face twisted in disgust. "You're too weak to be my mate. You can't even give me pups."

I'd believed him. How could I not? He was my fated mate, and he'd rejected me. My body had broken under the weight of that rejection, my cycle stopping, my scent diminishing. I'd believed I was damaged beyond repair.

But now...

"No," I whispered, shaking my head. "It can't be."

But instinct didn't lie. My wolf was already protective, already aware of the tiny spark of life growing within me. The wolf that had been dormant, wounded by rejection, was now alert and vigilant.

I was pregnant.

My knees buckled, and I slid to the floor, my back against the cool wooden cabinet. My breath came in short, panicked gasps as reality crashed over me.

I was carrying Kieran's pup.

A miracle I had thought impossible.

What would Kieran say when he found out? Would he be angry? Would he think I'd trapped him? Or worse—would he pretend to be happy only to reject me later, once the burden became too much?

I wrapped my arms around my stomach protectively. This pup—this impossible miracle—deserved better than an omega who'd been cast aside like garbage. Who was I to think I could be a parent when my own mate had found me unworthy?

But Kieran wasn't Callan. And then wasn't now, and there wasn't here.

In these weeks together, Kieran had shown me nothing but kindness, patience, and respect. He'd never forced me, never demanded anything I wasn't willing to give. He'd fed me, sheltered me, protected me—all without expectation.

Could I trust that? Could I trust him?

I didn't have a choice. This pup was his as much as mine. He deserved to know.

I pushed myself to my feet, splashing cold water on my face. My hand shook as I wiped away the tears. I had to tell him. Today. Now. Before I lost my courage.

I changed into clean clothes—a soft flannel shirt of Kieran's that hung past my thighs and a pair of borrowed sweatpants. His scent enveloped me, calming my racing heart slightly as I made my way to the kitchen.

Something drew me to the window first. The mountains stretched before me, snowcapped and eternal. Six months ago, I'd thought they would be my grave. Now they cradled the cabin where I'd found a second chance.

I was pouring myself a glass of water when I heard the front door open, bringing with it a gust of cold air and Kieran's scent. Pine, earth, and something uniquely him—a scent that had become synonymous with safety in my mind.

"Morning," he called, his voice deep and warm. I turned to watch him hang up his coat and remove his boots. Snow clung to his dark hair, and his cheeks were flushed from the cold. "There's a fresh layer of snow out there. At least another foot fell overnight."

I nodded, unable to find my voice. He must have sensed my distress because his smile faltered, concern creasing his brow.

"Rowan? What's wrong?" He crossed the room in three long strides, stopping just short of touching me. Always so careful. Always giving me space.

My enhanced senses caught the subtle changes in his scent—concern, protectiveness, a hint of fear. The bond between us thrummed with his worry.

I took a deep breath, my hands clutching the glass so tightly I feared it might shatter.

"I need to tell you something," I whispered, my voice barely audible even in the quiet cabin.

Kieran's silver eyes darkened with worry. "What is it? Are you feeling sick?"

I shook my head, fighting back a hysterical laugh. Sick? No. What I was feeling was as far from sickness as possible. It was life—impossible, miraculous life.

"I'm pregnant," I blurted out, the words hanging in the air between us.

Kieran froze. His entire body went still, his eyes widening, his lips parting slightly. The glass he'd been reaching for slipped from his fingers, shattering on the floor. Neither of us moved to clean it up.

I searched his face desperately, trying to read his expression. Shock, certainly, but what else? Anger? Dismay? Regret?

The silence stretched between us, unbearable and heavy. I couldn't take it anymore. I set down my glass with a shaking hand and turned away, tears blurring my vision once more.

"I understand if you don't... if this isn't what you..." I stumbled over the words, my throat tightening with each syllable. "I won't hold you to anything. I can leave once the snow melts—"

Strong arms wrapped around me from behind, pulling me against a solid chest. I gasped, my body tensing at the sudden contact.

"Rowan," Kieran breathed my name against my hair, his voice thick with emotion. "Rowan."

Just my name, over and over, like a prayer.

I turned in his arms, needing to see his face, to understand what was happening. What I saw stole my breath away.

Joy. Pure, undiluted joy shone in Kieran's eyes, transforming his features. He cupped my face in his large hands, his touch impossibly gentle as he stared down at me with wonder.

"You're pregnant," he whispered, as if saying it aloud might make it disappear. "We're having a pup."

I nodded, tears spilling freely now. "You're not... angry?"

His brow furrowed in confusion. "Angry? Why would I be angry about the greatest gift anyone has ever given me?"

I sobbed, my body shaking with the force of it as all the fear, the doubt, the pain of the past came pouring out.

Kieran held me through it, his arms a safe harbor as the storm of emotions raged through me. He pressed kisses to my hair, my forehead, my temple, murmuring words of comfort and amazement.

"I thought I would never have this," he confessed, his own voice rough with emotion. "A mate. A pup. A family. I resigned myself to being alone. And then you appeared in my forest, fierce and beautiful even as you fought for your life."

His hand drifted down to rest against my stomach, hesitating for a heartbeat before I nodded my permission. His fingers splayed across my abdomen, a protective gesture that made my heart constrict. The touch was reverent, almost worshipful.

"Mine," he growled softly, the sound more possessive than I'd ever heard from him. Not threatening—protective. Claiming. "Both of you, mine to protect. Mine to cherish."

The words should have frightened me, should have reminded me of Callan's controlling grip. Instead, they settled over me like a blanket, warm and secure. Because Kieran's possession wasn't about control—it was about devotion.

"You have no idea how lucky I am," he whispered, pressing his forehead against mine. "To have found you. To be blessed with your trust, with your body's acceptance of my seed. This pup is a miracle, Rowan. You are a miracle."

I shook my head, overwhelmed by his words, by the raw emotion in his voice. "I'm broken," I whispered. "Callan said—"

"Callan was wrong." Kieran's voice hardened, a growl underlining his words. "He was blind and cruel and wrong. You are perfect, Rowan. Strong and resilient and beautiful. And you are carrying my pup, which makes you even more extraordinary in my eyes."

He guided me to a chair, kneeling before me. His hand

never left my stomach, as if he couldn't bear to break the connection to our child. His other hand took mine, thumb brushing over my knuckles.

"I didn't think I could conceive," I admitted, the words barely audible. "After the rejection... my body changed. I stopped cycling. I thought I was... damaged."

Kieran's eyes flashed, anger not at me but for me. "You were never damaged, Rowan. Your body was protecting you from further pain. But now..." His hand pressed gently against my abdomen. "Now, your body knows you're safe. It knows you're with your true mate."

True mate. Could it be true? Could I have been fated for Kieran all along?

"Don't you see what this means?" he asked, his voice gentle but insistent. "This pregnancy proves that Callan was never your true fated mate. If he had been, the rejection wouldn't have been possible. Your body wouldn't have accepted my seed so readily."

Throughout my relationship with Callan, conception had never occurred despite years together. Yet one heat with Kieran, and my body had responded as if it had been waiting for him all along.

"I'm scared," I confessed, burying my face against his chest. "What if something goes wrong? What if I can't... what if I'm not a good parent?"

Kieran's hand stroked my back, soothing circles that calmed my racing thoughts. "We'll figure it out together," he promised. "Every step of the way. You won't be alone in this, Rowan. Not ever again."

And for the first time since Callan had torn my world apart, I allowed myself to believe. To hope. To trust the feeling of rightness that settled over me as Kieran held me —us—in his protective embrace.

"I never thought I'd have this," I whispered, echoing his earlier words. "A second chance. A true mate. A pup."

Kieran tilted my chin up, his eyes meeting mine with an intensity that stole my breath. "You deserve all of it and more," he said fiercely. "And I will spend the rest of my life making sure you never doubt that again."

He kissed me then, a gentle press of lips that conveyed more than words ever could. A promise. A vow. A future.

I felt it then—a tiny flutter in my abdomen, too early to be the pup moving but something more primal. My wolf recognizing the new life, acknowledging it, protecting it.

"We're going to be parents," I whispered against Kieran's lips, testing the words, finding they felt right. True.

Kieran smiled, the expression transforming his rugged features into something breathtaking. "Yes," he agreed, his hand splayed protectively over my tummy. "And we're going to be amazing."

I was carrying proof that I had never been broken. Just waiting for the right alpha to see my worth.

CHAPTER 8

I stood at the window of my cabin, watching the snow gently fall as dawn broke over the mountains. My wolf paced with contentment beneath my skin, a low rumble of satisfaction vibrating in my chest. *Rowan. Mine. Safe. Ours.* The knowledge that he carried my pup made my protective instincts flare even stronger.

I heard Rowan's footsteps before I felt his presence behind me. He didn't touch me—he rarely initiated contact —but he stood close enough that I could feel his warmth.

"The storm's letting up," he said, his voice still rough with sleep.

I nodded. "Spring's coming. Another few weeks and the worst of winter will be behind us."

What I didn't say was that the clearer weather would make travel easier. I didn't want to remind him that he could leave if he wanted to, though the very thought made my wolf growl in protest. Not now. Not with our pup growing inside him.

"I was thinking," I said carefully, turning to face him,

"that we should radio Elias and the others. Let them know about..." I gestured vaguely to his midsection.

Rowan tensed, wrapping his arms around himself protectively. "Your pack."

"They're good people, Rowan. They'll be happy for us."

His eyes darted away. "They'll think I trapped you."

I couldn't stop myself from reaching for him then, gently tilting his chin up until those golden eyes met mine. "No one who knows me would ever think I could be trapped against my will."

A ghost of a smile touched his lips. Progress.

"Besides," I continued, "Sawyer should check you both over. He's a skilled healer."

Rowan hesitated, then gave a small nod. It wasn't enthusiastic, but it was agreement. Another small victory.

I was about to suggest breakfast when I felt it—a prickling sensation at the back of my neck. My wolf suddenly went rigid, senses sharpening. Someone was approaching. Someone who didn't belong.

The birds outside fell silent. The forest itself seemed to hold its breath. A cold feeling settled in the pit of my stomach—not just wariness, but primal recognition of a threat.

I moved to the door, my body blocking the entrance as I stared out into the forest. I could feel my features shifting slightly, becoming more wolf-like as my canines lengthened and my eyes sharpened. Rowan noticed the change immediately.

"Kieran? What is it?"

I inhaled deeply, sorting through the scents carried on the crisp mountain air. Pine. Snow. The lingering smoke from our chimney. And then—

My lips pulled back in a snarl, a growl erupting from deep in my chest.

"Another wolf," I growled, my voice barely recognizable. "Coming up the eastern path."

Rowan went completely still. "Just one?"

I nodded, straining my senses. "Just one. But..."

Before I could finish, Rowan's scent soured with fear—sharp and acrid, cutting through the sweet undertones that had developed since his pregnancy. His hand flew to his throat, an unconscious gesture I'd seen before when he spoke of his past.

"It's him," he whispered, and the terror in those two words made my blood boil.

"Callan."

I didn't need confirmation. The way Rowan's scent changed told me everything I needed to know. His heart rate spiked, the sound of it thundering in my ears. The wolf who had rejected him, who had thrown him away to die, had somehow tracked him here.

"Stay inside," I ordered, already reaching for my coat. "Lock the door behind me."

Rowan grabbed my arm, his fingers digging in with surprising strength. "No! What if he—"

"He won't," I cut him off, my voice hard with certainty. "Nothing is going to happen to you. Not while I'm breathing." I cupped his face, a gesture so natural now it surprised me how easily my body moved to comfort him. "I won't let him near you or our pup. I swear it."

"I don't want you to get hurt because of me," Rowan said, his voice small.

I almost laughed at the absurdity of it—the idea that I would be hurt by a wolf who couldn't even recognize the treasure he'd thrown away. "I need to meet him away from the cabin. Away from you." I let my thumb brush over his knuckles. "Trust me, Rowan. Please."

"Be careful," he whispered, his scent fluctuating between fear and something else—concern for me, I realized with a start.

I nodded, pulling on my coat and boots. At the door, I paused, looking back at him. "Lock the door behind me. Don't open it for anyone but me."

The air outside was sharp and clean, the silence broken only by the occasional drip of melting snow from the pine branches. I moved swiftly down the path, wanting to intercept Callan before he got too close to the cabin. Before he got too close to what was mine.

My wolf surged close to the surface, senses heightened to painful acuity. I could smell every animal for miles, hear the heartbeat of a rabbit hiding beneath the snow, feel the vibrations of footsteps approaching through the frozen ground.

I didn't have to wait long.

He emerged from between the trees like a shadow—tall, broad-shouldered, with hair as black as pitch. Even from a distance, I could see the imperious tilt of his head, the arrogance in his stance. This was a wolf used to being obeyed, used to taking what he wanted.

Not today.

I planted myself in the middle of the path, arms crossed over my chest, and waited. My stance was deliberate—territorial, protective, a clear warning to any wolf who understood our language. *Mine. My territory. My mate. My pup.*

He slowed as he spotted me, his head lifting to scent the air. Recognition flashed in his eyes—he knew exactly what I was to Rowan. His lips curled into a sneer.

"You must be the mountain recluse," he called, closing

the distance between us. "I've heard there was a lone alpha up here playing hermit. Didn't expect you to be poaching on my territory."

I remained perfectly still, letting him approach. "Your territory? Funny, I don't remember seeing your marks on these mountains." My voice dropped lower, a dangerous timbre entering it. "Or on the omega you abandoned."

That hit a nerve. His eyes flashed, a dangerous silver-gray. "Watch yourself, wolf. You don't know who you're dealing with."

"Callan Blackridge. Rising alpha of the Silverclaw Pack. Rejected his fated mate in front of his entire pack and left him to die." I smiled, but there was nothing friendly in it. "Did I miss anything?"

He stopped a few feet away from me, his nostrils flaring. "I've come for what's mine."

The casual possessiveness in his voice made my wolf surge forward, claws extending before I could stop them. I felt my face contort slightly, caught between human and wolf. I tamped it down, but only barely.

"Rowan doesn't belong to you," I said, my voice deadly calm. "You made sure of that when you severed the bond."

"A temporary setback," Callan dismissed with a wave of his hand. "I've reconsidered. The council agrees that the rejection can be reversed if both parties consent."

"Both parties?" I laughed, the sound harsh in the quiet forest. "You think after what you did, he'd ever consent to being yours again?"

Something ugly flashed across Callan's face. "He's an omega. He'll do what's best for him."

"And you think that's you?" I took a step forward, my control slipping. "You, who nearly killed him with your rejection? You, who left him to starve in these mountains?"

"He survived, didn't he?" Callan sneered. "Proves he's stronger than I thought. Worth keeping after all."

The casual cruelty of it struck me like a physical blow. This was the wolf who had held Rowan's heart in his hands and crushed it. This was the wolf who had looked at something precious and discarded it like trash.

I could smell it on him now—the taint of regret, not for hurting Rowan but for losing something he considered his possession. The stink of jealousy. The acrid scent of wounded pride.

"He more than survived," I said, my voice dropping to a dangerous rumble. "He thrived. He found what he was always meant to have."

Understanding dawned on Callan's face, followed by cold fury. "You claimed him," he hissed.

I said nothing, letting my silence answer for me. A slight smile played at my lips, the satisfaction of knowing Rowan was mine—by choice, not by force—warming me despite the winter chill.

"Impossible." Callan shook his head, disbelief warring with rage. "The bond was severed. He was damaged goods."

My control snapped.

I lunged forward, seizing him by the throat and slamming him against the nearest tree. The bark cracked under the impact, bits of ice and snow raining down around us. Callan's eyes widened in shock as my fingers tightened around his windpipe.

"Say that again," I growled, my wolf so close to the surface I could feel my canines lengthening, my eyes shifting to their wolf form. "Call him damaged one more time, and they'll find pieces of you scattered across three mountain ranges."

To his credit, Callan didn't cower. Even as he struggled for breath, his lips curved into a mocking smile.

"Protective," he wheezed. "But it changes nothing. You can't mate what's already been marked."

I released him abruptly, stepping back as he slumped against the tree, rubbing his throat.

"That's where you're wrong," I said quietly. "Fate doesn't make mistakes, Callan. Rowan was never meant to be yours. You were just a detour on his path to me."

Callan straightened, his eyes narrowing. "Let me see him."

I stilled, every instinct screaming at me to refuse. To drive this threat away from my mate, my unborn child. But I knew I couldn't make this decision for Rowan. He needed to face his past to truly move forward.

"Why should I?" I challenged.

"An omega has the right to hear a formal retraction of rejection," Callan said, his voice taking on an official tone. "It's pack law."

"You threw away pack law when you abandoned him to die," I countered. "But fine. You want to see him? You can see him. But understand this—" I stepped closer, my voice dropping to a whisper only another wolf could hear. "If he wants you gone, you go. Immediately. Or I will tear out your throat, council be damned."

Something flashed in Callan's eyes—perhaps the first hint of uncertainty. Good. He should be afraid.

"Lead the way," he said, his voice tight.

I turned and started back toward the cabin, every sense hyper-focused on the wolf behind me. I could feel his anticipation, his certainty that Rowan would choose him.

Fool.

As we neared the cabin, I caught a flicker of movement

at the window. Rowan. I could sense his fear even from here, a sour note in the air that made my wolf growl protectively. But beneath it, I caught something else—determination. Strength.

Halfway to the cabin, I felt it—a strange sensation deep in my gut. The mate bond between Rowan and me pulsed, almost painfully intense. It took me a moment to recognize what was happening. Rowan was reaching for me through the bond, drawing on my strength. Preparing himself.

Pride surged through me. Even terrified, even faced with the wolf who had broken him, Rowan was standing his ground. Fighting.

I stopped at the foot of the porch steps, turning to Callan. "Remember what I said. His choice."

Callan's jaw tightened, but he nodded once.

When we reached the door, I knocked gently. "Rowan, it's me. Open the door."

There was a moment of hesitation before the lock clicked and the door swung open. Rowan stood there, his chin lifted in defiance despite the fear I could smell coming off him in waves. One hand rested protectively over his stomach—a gesture so subtle that only the most observant wolf would notice, but one that sent a jolt of fierce joy through me.

His eyes met mine first, questioning, seeking reassurance. Then they shifted to Callan, and I watched as a complex mix of emotions crossed his face—fear, pain, anger, and finally, a steely resolve that made my chest swell with pride.

"Hello, Callan," he said, his voice steady. "I wish I could say it's good to see you."

In that moment, I knew. Whatever happened next, Rowan had already won. The broken omega Callan had cast aside no longer existed. In his place stood my mate—strong, defiant, and carrying the future of our pack within him.

I moved to stand beside him, not possessively, but protectively. A silent promise that whatever came next, he wouldn't face it alone. Rowan's hand brushed against mine, a brief touch but deliberate. A choice. His choice.

And for the first time since sensing Callan's approach, my wolf settled, content in the knowledge that what was ours was safe. Not because I would protect it, though I would die doing so if necessary. But because Rowan was strong enough to protect himself.

CHAPTER 9

I knew that scent.

It hit me like a physical blow—wild pine, mountain stone, and that sharp undertone of dominance that had once made my knees weak. Now it just made my stomach clench.

Callan.

My hand instinctively went to my abdomen, a protective gesture that happened before I could even think about it. My baby. Kieran's baby. The miracle I never thought possible after what Callan had done to me.

I forced myself to breathe as the two alphas entered the cabin. Kieran moved to stand beside me, not possessively, but protectively—a silent promise that I wasn't alone. The contrast between the two alphas had never been clearer than in this moment.

"Hello, Callan," I said, my voice steadier than I expected. "I wish I could say it's good to see you."

Callan's eyes swept over me, cataloging the changes since he'd last seen me. I wasn't the same broken omega he'd cast out. I stood taller, my body no longer emaciated from rejection sickness, my eyes no longer dull with despair.

"Rowan," he said, and there was something like wonder in his voice. "You look... different."

"Healthy," I corrected. "I look healthy."

He took a step toward me, and I forced myself not to retreat. I wouldn't show weakness. Not anymore.

"I've come to bring you home," he announced, as if conferring a great honor. "The pack misses you. I..." He hesitated, then pushed on. "I made a mistake. The rejection was hasty, ill-considered."

I stared at him for a long moment, disbelief written across my features.

"A mistake," I repeated flatly. "Humiliating me in front of the entire pack was a 'mistake'? Telling everyone I was too weak to be your mate was a 'mistake'?"

Callan had the grace to look uncomfortable. "I was under pressure. The council, the expectations... I wasn't thinking clearly."

"And now you are?" My laugh was brittle. "Now that someone else wants me, suddenly I'm worth having again?"

"It's not like that," Callan protested, but his eyes betrayed him. He glanced at Kieran, then back to me with newfound intensity. "The bond can be restored. We can start over, as we were meant to."

"As we were meant to," I echoed, and I heard the tremor in my voice. This was costing me, standing up to the wolf who had once meant everything to me.

I took a steadying breath, drawing strength from Kieran's presence at my side.

"You know what I've realized, Callan?" I continued, my voice growing stronger. "We were never meant to be. Fate doesn't make mistakes—but people do. You made a choice. You threw me away."

Callan's facade of contrition slipped, revealing the anger beneath. "And you ran straight into the arms of the first alpha who would have you. How convenient."

Kieran growled low in his throat, but I placed a hand on his arm—the first time I had willingly touched him in front of another person. The simple gesture silenced him instantly.

"I nearly died because of you," I said, and the quiet dignity in my voice made Callan flinch. "I fought every day to survive, alone, while you lived comfortably with our pack. And now you have the audacity to come here and claim me as if I'm a lost possession?"

Callan's eyes narrowed. "You're being dramatic. You were always too emotional, too—"

"Careful," Kieran warned, unable to stay silent any longer.

But I squeezed his arm, my touch anchoring him.

"Do you have any idea what it was like?" I asked, stepping forward, away from Kieran's protective presence, standing on my own. "Feeling our bond shatter? Having your contempt pour through what was left of it? I felt every ounce of your disgust, your disappointment."

My voice shook, but I pushed on. "I lay on the forest floor for three days after I left. Too weak to hunt. Too weak to even find water. Do you know what kept me alive? Spite. The absolute refusal to let you be right about me being too weak."

Callan's expression flickered between surprise and anger. "Rowan—"

"I crawled. I dragged myself to water. I caught fish with my bare hands when I couldn't even stand up straight. I survived six months alone in these mountains with nothing but the clothes on my back."

Pride swelled in my chest—not the toxic pride that had driven Callan to reject me, but something purer. Pride in my own strength. My own resilience.

"I never needed your protection, Callan. And I certainly don't need it now."

For the first time, uncertainty crossed his face. He hadn't expected this—the omega who'd once hung on his every word now standing defiant before him.

"You've changed," he said, almost accusingly.

"I've healed," I corrected him. "Despite what you did to me."

He glanced at Kieran, his eyes narrowing. "Because of him? Some alpha who found you weak and desperate? Is that what this is about—gratitude?"

The laugh that bubbled up from my chest surprised even me. "You still don't understand, do you? Kieran didn't 'find' me. He recognized me. As his fated mate."

The shock on Callan's face would have been satisfying if it wasn't quickly replaced by fury. "That's impossible. You can't have two fated mates."

"Apparently I can," I said. "And this one didn't throw me away."

"The bond never fully broke," Callan insisted, desperation edging into his voice. "That's why I can still feel you. That's why I tracked you here. You're still mine."

"No," I said, the single word feeling like a victory. "I wasn't meant to be yours. If I had been, you wouldn't have been able to reject me."

"It was a mistake!" Callan's voice rose, his control slipping. "One I'm trying to fix!"

"It wasn't a mistake," I said, my voice growing stronger

with each word. "It was a choice. Your choice. And it nearly killed me."

Callan's eyes darted to my stomach, the movement so quick I almost missed it. "There's more, isn't there? Something you're not telling me."

I exchanged a glance with Kieran, who nodded slightly. There was no point hiding it.

"I'm pregnant," I said simply.

Callan went still, his eyes widening as they fixed on my abdomen.

"That's not possible," he whispered. "Rejection sickness causes infertility. Everyone knows that."

"Apparently not," I said quietly, one hand resting protectively over my abdomen. "The healer confirmed it yesterday."

Something crumpled in Callan's expression—the final blow to his pride, to his certainty that he could simply reclaim what he'd thrown away.

"You're lying," he said, but the words lacked conviction.

"I have no reason to lie to you, Callan. I owe you nothing."

"You were always mine," he growled, desperation making him dangerous. "You'll always be mine!"

He lunged toward me with unexpected speed. But before I could even flinch, Kieran was there, intercepting him mid-lunge and slamming him against the wall with enough force to rattle the shelves.

"You've had your say," Kieran growled, his forearm pressed against Callan's throat. "Now you'll leave. Peacefully. Or I'll tear out your throat and deal with the consequences later."

The two alphas stared at each other, locked in silent combat. I could see Callan calculating his odds, weighing his pride against Kieran's obvious willingness to kill for me.

"Kieran," I said softly. "Let him go."

Kieran hesitated, then slowly released his grip, stepping back to stand beside me but remaining tensed, ready to move if Callan made another lunge.

But the fight seemed to have gone out of my former mate. He stared at me, really seeing me for perhaps the first time.

"This isn't over, Rowan," he said, but the threat sounded hollow.

"Yes, it is." I reached for Kieran's hand, our fingers intertwining. The simple touch sent warmth cascading through me, our bond humming with contentment. "I've made my choice. And it isn't you."

"The pack won't accept this," Callan threatened, but his voice had lost its conviction. "An omega with two alphas— it's unheard of."

"I don't have two alphas," I corrected him. "I have one. The one who saw me at my weakest and still believed I was strong. The one who gave me space when I needed it and protection when I asked for it."

I looked up at Kieran, finding strength in the steady silver of his gaze. "The one who never once made me feel like I had to earn my place at his side."

Callan's jaw tightened. For a moment, I thought he might argue further, might try to force the issue. But something in our united front must have gotten through to him. With a final, burning glare, he turned and stalked toward the door.

At the threshold, he paused, looking back over his shoulder. "When this falls apart—when you realize you've made a mistake—don't come crawling back to me."

I almost laughed at the absurdity of it. "I didn't crawl to you when I was dying from rejection sickness. I won't crawl to you ever again."

The door slammed behind him with enough force to shake dust from the rafters. In the sudden silence, I could hear my own heartbeat, rapid but strong.

Kieran's arms came around me from behind, gentle but secure. "Are you alright?"

I leaned back against his chest, feeling the steady thud of his heart against my back. "I think I am. For the first time in a very long time."

His hand came to rest over mine on my stomach, our fingers intertwining to protect the tiny miracle growing inside me. "You were magnificent," he murmured, pressing a kiss to my temple.

"I was terrified," I admitted.

"Being brave isn't about not feeling fear," Kieran said. "It's about facing it anyway."

I turned in his arms, looking up into those silver eyes that had become my anchor in a storm-tossed sea. "Do you think he'll come back? With others?"

Kieran's expression hardened slightly. "If he does, he'll find more than just me waiting for him. My pack protects our own."

Our own. The words settled around me like a blanket, warm and secure.

"What if he's right?" I asked, voicing the fear that still lingered despite everything. "What if an omega can't have two fated mates?"

"You don't have two alphas," Kieran said, echoing my earlier words. "You had one who didn't deserve you. And now you have one who will spend every day trying to be worthy of you."

He pressed his forehead against mine, our breaths mingling. "The old bond is broken, Rowan. Completely and irrevocably broken the moment our new one formed. That's why you could conceive. That's why you're healing."

"How can you be so sure?" I whispered.

His hand cupped my cheek, thumb tracing the line of my cheekbone with infinite tenderness. "Because fate doesn't make mistakes, little wolf. You were never meant for him. You were always meant for me."

CHAPTER 10

My heart was still racing from yesterday's confrontation. The words I'd spoken to him—words I never thought I'd have the courage to say—echoed in my mind.

You threw me away. I belong to no one but myself—and the mate who actually wanted me.

Even now, I could hardly believe I'd said it. That I'd stood my ground against the alpha who had once been my world. The alpha who had rejected me in front of our entire pack, severing our bond and leaving me to die in the wilderness.

Kieran moved beside me, his warmth radiating against my side without touching me. He'd been doing that since yesterday—staying close but giving me space, as if he knew I needed to process everything that had happened.

"Are you cold?" he asked, his deep voice rumbling through the crisp morning air.

I shook my head. "No. Just thinking."

His silver eyes studied me, concern etched in the slight furrow of his brow. "About Callan?"

"About everything," I admitted. "About how different my life is now compared to six months ago."

Six months ago, I had been cast out, rejected, humiliated. Six months ago, I had been certain I would die alone in these mountains. And now...

My hand pressed more firmly against my still-flat stomach. Now I was carrying a child. Kieran's child. A miracle I never thought possible after the rejection sickness had ravaged my body.

"I can smell them," Kieran said suddenly, lifting his head and sniffing the air. "My pack. They're coming."

A cold wave of anxiety washed over me. I'd faced Callan, yes, but facing an entire pack? Even if it was Kieran's pack, the memory of my last pack experience was still raw—their faces twisted with disgust as Callan proclaimed me unworthy to be his mate.

"Rowan." Kieran's voice pulled me from the memory. He hadn't touched me, but his presence was solid, grounding. "They're coming to help, not to judge. But if you're not ready..."

"No," I said, squaring my shoulders. "I need to meet them. I need to—" I swallowed hard, searching for the right words. "I need to know if they'll accept me. Us." My hand remained protectively over my stomach.

Kieran's eyes softened. "They will."

"How can you be so sure?" The words came out more bitter than I intended. "Your last pack sure as hell didn't want a broken omega."

"You're not broken," Kieran growled, and for the first time that morning, he reached for me, his large hand enveloping mine. "And they're nothing like your old pack. Nothing like Callan."

I wanted to believe him. God, how I wanted to believe

that there were wolves who wouldn't see me as weak, as a burden, as unworthy. But hope was a dangerous thing for someone who had survived on nothing but bitter determination for so long.

"There they are," Kieran said, nodding toward the tree line.

Five wolves emerged from the forest, shifting from their wolf forms to human as they approached the cabin. The transition was fluid, natural—nothing like the desperate, painful shifts I'd endured in the months after my rejection when my body had fought against itself.

I tensed as they approached, instinctively moving closer to Kieran. His hand squeezed mine gently, a silent reassurance.

The first to reach us was a tall, dark-skinned man with short dreadlocks and amber eyes that seemed to take in everything at once. He moved with the confident grace of a high-ranking wolf, and I immediately identified him as Kieran's second.

"Elias," Kieran greeted him with a nod.

Elias's gaze moved from Kieran to me, and I braced myself for the judgment, the disgust, the pity. Instead, his expression shifted to something that looked almost like... respect?

"Omega," he said, inclining his head in a slight bow. "It's an honor to meet Kieran's mate."

The formality of the greeting caught me off guard. In my old pack, omegas were rarely addressed with such deference, especially not a rejected one.

"I—" My voice caught. "Thank you."

A lean wolf with golden-brown hair and mischievous green eyes stepped forward next, a grin spreading across his face. "So this is the one who finally caught our reclusive alpha. I was beginning to think he'd die alone in these mountains." He extended his hand. "I'm Theo."

I hesitated before taking it, half-expecting some trick, but his grip was firm and sincere.

"Ignore him," said a sandy-blond man with kind brown eyes, pushing Theo aside gently. "I'm Sawyer, the pack healer." His gaze was assessing but not invasive. "Kieran said you were injured by a mountain lion? And that Callan was here yesterday?"

I nodded, uncomfortable with the scrutiny but appreciating the concern in his tone.

"I'd like to check your wounds, if that's alright," Sawyer continued. "And—" He paused, his eyes flickering briefly to my hand still resting on my stomach.

My heart stuttered. Could he tell? Already?

The last two wolves introduced themselves—a fiery redhead named Luca who seemed wary, his blue eyes darting between Kieran and me as if trying to work out a puzzle, and a short but clearly formidable woman with black curls named Nadia, whose protective stance reminded me of a mother wolf guarding her den.

"Let's go inside," Kieran suggested, his hand moving to the small of my back, not pushing, just a presence. "It's warmer, and we have things to discuss."

The cabin suddenly felt much smaller with seven people inside it. I found myself retreating to the corner near the fireplace, a position that gave me a clear view of everyone while keeping my back protected—a habit developed during my months in the wild.

Elias spoke first, once everyone had settled. "Callan returned to the Silverclaw territory. He was... displeased."

"Good," Kieran growled, his posture tense. "If he comes back, he won't leave in one piece."

"Kieran," Elias said, his tone cautious, "you know what this means. The Silverclaw Pack won't take this lying down. Not after their alpha was humiliated."

"Let them come," Kieran replied, his voice deadly calm. "They threw Rowan away. They don't get to change their minds now."

The casual confidence in his voice sent a strange warmth through me. No one had ever defended me like this before, with such absolute certainty.

"I don't want to cause trouble for your pack," I said quietly, drawing all eyes to me. "Maybe it would be better if I—"

"No," Kieran cut me off, his silver eyes flashing. "You're not going anywhere."

"We can handle the Silverclaws," Theo added with a cocky grin. "They're all show and no bite. Always have been."

Luca, who had been silent until now, spoke up. "What if they come in full force? We're outnumbered."

"We have alliances," Nadia reminded him. "And territory advantages. This is our mountain."

I watched them discuss strategies and contingencies, feeling strangely disconnected from it all. These wolves, who barely knew me, were preparing to defend me against my former pack. Against Callan.

"It doesn't matter," I said suddenly, my voice stronger than I expected. "Callan won't stop. Not until he gets what he wants."

"And what does he want?" Sawyer asked gently.

I met his gaze. "To prove he was right. That I was unworthy. That no one else would want me either."

The room fell silent, and I could feel Kieran's eyes on me, intense and unwavering.

"Well, he failed spectacularly at that," Theo finally said, breaking the tension with a laugh. "Look at you—claimed by one of the strongest alphas in the northern territory. That's got to sting."

A reluctant smile tugged at my lips. "I suppose it does."

"Sawyer," Kieran said, changing the subject, "would you check Rowan's injuries? And..." He hesitated, his eyes meeting mine in silent question.

I nodded slowly. They needed to know. All of them.

"And confirm his condition," Kieran finished.

Sawyer's eyebrows rose slightly, but he nodded. "Of course. Would you prefer privacy, Omega?"

The respectful question, so different from the invasive examinations I'd endured in my old pack, caught me off guard.

"No," I decided after a moment. "They should all know."

The others looked confused, but they remained silent as Sawyer approached me. His touch was clinical but gentle as he examined the healing claw marks on my shoulder from the mountain lion attack.

"These are healing well," he murmured. "Kieran did a good job with them."

Then he crouched in front of me, his hands hovering over my midsection. "May I?"

I nodded, my heart pounding.

Sawyer placed his hands lightly on my stomach, his eyes closing in concentration. As a healer, he could sense things other wolves couldn't—subtle changes in energy, in life force. I held my breath as his hands moved slowly over my abdomen, his expression shifting from concentration to surprise.

When he looked up at me, his eyes were wide. "You're carrying Kieran's pup."

The words hung in the air, solid and irrefutable. I heard several gasps, felt the weight of everyone's stares.

"That's impossible," Luca blurted out. "He was rejected. Rejection sickness makes omegas infertile."

"Usually," Sawyer agreed, standing up. "But not always. Especially not when they find their true fated mate." He turned to Kieran. "This isn't just any pup, Kieran. The life force is strong. Very strong."

Kieran moved to my side, his presence solid and unwavering. "I know," he said simply.

Elias was the first to approach us, his amber eyes solemn. "This changes things. A pregnant omega... Callan will see it as the ultimate insult."

"I don't care what Callan thinks," Kieran replied. "Rowan is my mate. The pup is mine. Nothing else matters."

"It's more than that," Nadia said, stepping forward. Her blue eyes met mine directly. "A pup conceived after rejection sickness... it's rare. Some would call it a blessing from the moon herself."

I blinked at her, unsure how to respond. In my old pack, my pregnancy would have been seen as a fluke, an accident, perhaps even something to be ashamed of. But the way Nadia spoke—with reverence, with awe—it was unsettling.

"What she means," Theo clarified with a grin, "is that you're officially the most badass omega any of us have ever met."

A startled laugh escaped me, breaking some of the tension in the room.

"I still don't understand," I admitted, looking around at these strangers who were discussing my pregnancy as if it were something miraculous. "In my pack, omegas were just... vessels. Useful, but replaceable."

The silence that followed my words was heavy with something I couldn't quite identify.

"Your pack was wrong," Sawyer said finally, his voice gentle but firm. "Omegas are the heart of any pack. They bring balance, nurturing, and strength of a different kind."

"The Silverclaw Pack has always been known for their outdated views," Elias added. "It's why they're isolated, why few packs align with them."

I looked at each of them in turn—Elias with his quiet strength, Theo with his easy smile, Sawyer with his gentle wisdom, Luca with his cautious curiosity, and Nadia with her fierce protectiveness. None of them looked at me with disgust or pity. None of them seemed to see me as weak or unworthy.

And then I looked at Kieran, whose silver eyes had never left me, whose presence had been a constant anchor since he'd found me bleeding and half-dead in the forest.

"So what happens now?" I asked, my voice barely above a whisper.

It was Kieran who answered, his voice certain. "Now you rest. You heal. You grow strong again." His hand reached for mine, and this time I didn't hesitate to take it. "And we protect what's ours."

"We protect what's ours," Elias echoed, and one by one, the others repeated the phrase—a vow, a promise, a welcome.

It was the beginning of everything.

EPILOGUE - ONE YEAR LATER

I stood by the handcrafted crib, watching our three-month-old son sleep peacefully, his tiny chest rising and falling with each breath. Aiden had Kieran's dark hair but my golden eyes, a perfect blend of us both.

"You're going to wear a hole in the floor with all that hovering," came Kieran's sleep-rough voice from our bed.

I turned, a smile tugging at my lips. "I can't help it. Sometimes I still can't believe he's real."

Kieran pushed himself up, the blankets pooling around his waist, revealing the muscled chest I'd mapped with my fingers a thousand times since that first desperate heat. "Come back to bed. He'll be up demanding attention soon enough."

But I couldn't tear myself away from our miracle. My fingers gently brushed Aiden's soft cheek, marveling at how something so perfect could exist in a world that had once been so cruel.

A year ago, I'd been starving and dying in these same mountains, rejected and discarded by a mate who found me wanting. Now I stood in a home filled with warmth, with a bond so strong it had created life, watching over a child I'd never dared to dream possible.

The floor creaked as Kieran padded across the room to join me, his strong arms encircling my waist from behind, his chin resting on my shoulder as we both gazed down at our son.

"You're thinking too loud," he murmured, pressing a kiss to the sensitive spot where my neck met my shoulder—right over his claiming mark.

"Just remembering," I admitted, leaning back into his solid warmth. "Where I was a year ago. How I never thought I'd have any of this."

His arms tightened around me. "And now?"

"Now I can't imagine any other life."

It hadn't been easy. After Callan's departure, after the pack's acceptance, after discovering the pregnancy—there had still been nightmares. Moments of panic. Days when I was certain Kieran would wake up and realize he'd made a terrible mistake.

But he never did.

He had been there through the morning sickness that lasted well into the afternoon. Through the night terrors that had me crying out, reliving the moment Callan had renounced me in front of his entire pack. Through the moments when my body changed so rapidly I barely recognized myself.

"Remember when Sawyer told us it was a boy?" Kieran asked, his voice soft with the memory.

I laughed quietly. "You strutted around for days like you'd personally arranged it."

"I was proud," he defended himself, nuzzling against my hair. "I am proud. Of him. Of you."

Those words still had the power to make my heart stutter, even after hearing them countless times over the past year. For someone who had been told they were worthless, hearing *proud* spoken with such conviction was like rainfall on parched earth.

Aiden stirred in his crib, his tiny face scrunching before settling again into peaceful sleep.

"He looks like you when he does that," Kieran said, amusement coloring his voice.

"What, frowning? I don't frown that much."

"You do when you're concentrating. When you're stalking prey. When you're about to win at cards against Theo."

I smiled at the mention of Kieran's packmate. Theo had appointed himself Aiden's favorite uncle and visited more often than anyone, always bringing some ridiculous gift and outrageous stories.

The pack had become my family in a way I'd never experienced. Elias with his quiet strength, Sawyer with his gentle healing hands, Nadia with her fierce protectiveness, and even Luca, who had gone from suspicious to stubbornly loyal once he'd seen me stand up to Callan.

"Do you want to know my favorite moment from this past year?" I asked, turning in Kieran's arms to face him.

He raised an eyebrow, curiosity bright in his silver eyes. "Tell me."

"It was after Aiden was born. You were holding him, and you looked... terrified." I reached up to trace the scar along his jaw. "This powerful alpha who had faced down mountain lions and rival packs, completely undone by seven pounds of newborn."

Kieran's laugh rumbled in his chest. "He was so small. I was convinced I'd break him."

"But you didn't. You just kept holding him, looking at him like he was the most precious thing you'd ever seen."

"He is," Kieran said simply. "He and you."

It was still overwhelming sometimes, the depth of emotion in his voice when he said things like that. The complete absence of doubt. The certainty that I belonged here, with him.

"There was a moment," I confessed, my voice dropping to barely a whisper, "right after Aiden was born, when I thought...*what if he grows up and someone rejects him the way Callan rejected me?*"

Kieran's hands came up to cup my face, his eyes fierce. "That will never happen."

"You can't know that."

"I can. Because he'll grow up knowing exactly how powerful he is. How worthy. How deeply he's loved. And if anyone ever tries to make him feel less than that, he'll have an entire pack to remind him of the truth."

My throat tightened with emotion. "The way they did for me."

"The way they did for you," he agreed. "The way I always will."

I thought of the first time Kieran's pack had visited after learning of my pregnancy. How they had arrived bearing gifts and food, how they had touched my stomach with reverent hands, how they had promised protection for a child who wasn't even born yet.

I thought of Nadia teaching me to fight even as my belly grew, insisting that no omega in her pack would ever be defenseless. Of Sawyer checking on me weekly, bringing herbs and tinctures to ease the pregnancy symptoms. Of Elias constructing the crib that now held our son, carving protective runes into the wood.

"I never expected to find a family," I admitted. "When I was running from Callan, from the rejection, all I wanted was to survive. To prove I wasn't as weak as he claimed."

"And instead, you found us," Kieran said, a smile spreading across his face.

"Instead, I found you," I corrected, rising on my toes to press a kiss to his lips. "Everything else followed."

And it had. The cabin that had once been just a shelter from a snowstorm had become a home filled with laughter and warmth. The territory that had nearly killed me had become the land where I hunted and thrived. The alpha who had saved me from a mountain lion had become the mate who saved me from loneliness.

From the crib, a small whimper sounded, quickly building into a hungry cry. Aiden was awake, his tiny fists waving in the air as his face reddened with effort.

"Someone knows we're talking about him," Kieran said, releasing me so I could lift our son.

Aiden's cries immediately softened as I cradled him against my chest, his golden eyes—so like mine—blinking up at me with complete trust.

"Good morning, little wolf," I murmured, feeling the now-familiar surge of love that came whenever I held him. "Did you sleep well?"

He made a gurgling sound in response, his tiny hand reaching up to grasp at my finger with surprising strength. Another trait from his alpha father.

"He's going to be as stubborn as you," Kieran observed, watching us with naked adoration.

"Good. He'll need it in this family." I smiled down at our son. "Won't you, Aiden? With Uncle Theo trying to teach you pranks and Uncle Luca showing you how to pick fights."

"And his papa showing him how to win them," Kieran added with a grin.

I moved to the rocking chair by the window, settling in to feed Aiden. The morning light streamed over us, warm and golden. Below our cabin, the valley stretched out in spring glory, wildflowers dotting the meadows where the pack would run during the next full moon.

Kieran knelt beside the rocking chair, one hand gently stroking Aiden's dark hair as he nursed. "I've been thinking," he said, his voice thoughtful.

"Dangerous," I teased.

He pinched my side playfully. "I'm serious. The cabin's getting small for the three of us. And if we wanted to expand our family someday..."

My heart skipped a beat. "You want more children?"

"I want whatever you want," he said simply. "But yes, I think Aiden would make an excellent big brother. Not right away," he added hastily, noting my wide eyes. "But someday. When you're ready."

A year ago, the idea of being a parent at all had been inconceivable. Now, looking down at our son, the possibility of giving him siblings someday felt right. Natural.

"I think I'd like that," I said softly. "Someday."

Kieran's face lit up with a smile that still made my knees weak. "In the meantime, I thought we might add onto the cabin. A bigger kitchen, maybe another bedroom. A proper playroom for when he's older."

"You're nesting," I observed, laughing quietly.

"I'm planning," he corrected, touching my cheek. "For our future. For a life where Aiden grows up surrounded by love and pack and family."

The life I'd never had. The life I'd never dared to dream of for myself.

"I love you," I said, the words coming easily now after months of practice, months of learning that vulnerability wasn't weakness.

Kieran leaned forward, pressing his forehead to mine. "I love you too. Both of you."

Aiden made a small noise between us, as if agreeing with his father's sentiment.

Outside our window, birds called to each other in the pine trees. The mountains that had once been my prison now stood as the boundaries of our territory, protecting rather than confining. The wilderness that had nearly claimed my life had become the place where I found everything I'd ever wanted.

"We're going to be late for the pack gathering if we don't start getting ready," Kieran reminded me gently.

Today was Aiden's formal introduction to the extended pack—wolves from neighboring territories who had allied with Kieran over the years. It was a ceremony I'd never experienced myself, having been rejected before such an event could take place in Callan's pack.

"They're going to love him," Kieran said, reading the momentary anxiety in my face. "Almost as much as we do."

I looked down at Aiden, now drowsily content after feeding, his tiny hand still wrapped around my finger as if he'd never let go.

"I know," I said, and I meant it. Because this pack, unlike my old one, saw strength in connection rather than dominance. They valued bonds that ran deeper than blood.

I rose from the rocking chair, holding Aiden securely against my shoulder. "Come on, little one. Time to get you dressed for your big day."

Kieran wrapped his arms around us both, creating a circle of warmth and protection. In the quiet of our bedroom, with morning light streaming through the windows and our son nestled between us, I finally understood what home truly meant.

It wasn't the cabin, though I loved every board and beam. It wasn't the territory, though I'd learned to thrive in its wilderness. It wasn't even the pack, though they had become the family I'd never known I needed.

Home was this—the beat of Kieran's heart against mine, the weight of Aiden in my arms, the knowledge that no matter what happened, I would never face it alone again.

I had been cast out, rejected, and left to die. But fate had other plans. Fate had led me to a mountain lion, to a silver-eyed alpha, to a bond that couldn't be denied.

Fate had led me home.

THE END

THANK you for reading my book! I would love to hear what you think, please leave me a review or drop me a line at AshlynDupree@gmail.com.

Printed in Dunstable, United Kingdom